HORIZONTAL RAIN

U.H Dematagoda

HYPERIDEAN PRESS

Edinburgh

Copyright © 2020 by U.H Dematagoda

All rights reserved. No part of this publication may be reproduced, distributed or transmitted in any form or by any means, without prior written permission.

Hyperidean Press
Pilrig Street Edinburgh
www.hyperideanpress.com

Publisher's Note: This is a work of fiction. Any resemblance found to real persons, entities, institutions and events is purely coincidental.

Stewart McCarthy & Richard Porteous – Editors
Jamie Sunderland – Design and Art Direction

Cover Artwork: Strawberry Moon on Iona (2018) by Sean Patrick Campbell

Horizontal Rain/ U.H Dematagoda. – First Edition August 2020

ISBN 978-1-9163767-4-8

For my friends

The self does not care whether one is cast of bronze or the heart has an iron lining. At night the self only desires to steep its clangour in softness, in woman.

– Vladimir Mayakovsky

I

FLESH IS WEAK

He felt an unfamiliar knot in his stomach as he slumped dejectedly down onto the old sofa, now bare of its soft throw covering, and lit a cigarette with a shaky hand. The decorative glass ashtray which had sat upon the coffee table, with mermaids adorning the sides, had already been boxed up. He flicked his ash into the teacup in front of him, and sighed impetuously. He glanced distractedly around the living room. This bare space, devoid of the little trinkets and decorations that had provided a palpable sense of familiar comfort, which he had undoubtedly taken for granted, now seemed wholly alien. Behind the door to the hallway, slightly ajar, came some faint sounds which were barely distinguishable from the all too oppressive silence; the crackle of tape being slowly yet deliberately pulled from the roll, the plastic rustle of bubble wrap being pushed and folded into place; all punctuated with weak sobs, followed by sharp intakes of breath. In the far right hand corner of the room, there were a number of large cardboard boxes piled up high, sealed with plastic ties, but over-filled, and seemingly on the point of bursting open. This knot in his stomach had now developed into a mild pain, resonating just below his ribcage, and sending sharp chills down the length of his spine. He began to shiver uncontrollably. Outside of the window, the sun shone through unrelentingly, illuminating the bare white wall above the fireplace with an acrid orange glow. The cigarette had burned right down to the filter. He tossed it into the dregs of liquid in the mug, got to his feet, and walked over to the window. It was very warm that Saturday, and from the window of their flat, up on the third floor on the corner of Bentinck and Derby Street, he could observe several groups of people heading towards the entrance to Kelvingrove Park; groups of women pushing buggies or holding children, couples with dogs scampering about on leashes, bare-chested men holding shopping bags of beer, the red of their puckered flesh glowing uneasily under the rare sunlight. He took out his last cigarette and lit it. With a deliberate gesture he tipped the ash straight onto the beige carpet and rubbed it in with his foot.

The doorbell rang. He glanced over his shoulder as two removal men, the first who was tall, a little taller than himself but built far more solidly – the second, significantly shorter, but certainly wider on the ground, sauntered nonchalantly into the living room. They said nothing to him. They began lifting the boxes from the corner of the room, two at a time. One of the men, the taller of the two, was whistling a tune which, though familiar to him, he could not seem to place. In any case, it was certainly off key. The whole process took less than 10 minutes as they wandered in and out, grunting slightly, and lifting with incorrect and harmful posture. Outside, there was a small removal truck where a third man was loading the boxes onto the back. Afterwards he heard the front door close definitively – shaking the walls. On the coffee table, he could hear his phone vibrate. Out of the window, he could see the removal van pull off from the kerb, make a three-point-turn, and disappear around the corner at the opposite end of the street. The door to the living room creaked open, and he could hear her timid footsteps shuffle against the carpet. He didn't turn around.

'Is that everything then?'

'I'm going to leave some things here, I'll come and get them the next time I'm up. Is that cool?'

'Of course.'

'I left some cash on the kitchen table for the bills – it should be enough. I've left a little more, so you can buy some new sheets.'

'No need. I'll probably burn the bed and start sleeping on the floor.'

She giggled in a slightly affected manner – more from a sense of duty than anything else.

'When do you start work?' He asked.

'In two weeks, but I've got a lot things to sort out before then. And there's some training and orientation next week.'

'...'

'I don't know how to feel right now.'

'What time is the train?'

'...the taxi should be here in ten minutes.'

'Our last ten minutes together.'

'Don't say that.'

'I can say whatever I like...I'm the one being left alone.'

'I'll call you.'

'I won't answer.'

'You're being really childish.'

'Probably.'

'Just don't say things like that. Not right now. I can't imagine not being able to talk to you anymore.'

'Why? I have nothing new to say to you. I'm sure you'll get used to it.'

He could hear her breathing becoming more laboured and hoarse, followed by wet nasal sounds, attempts to catch her breath, stuttering. After some moments, it was quite clear that she had begun to cry. He felt an almost irrepressible urge to do or say something to make her stop, but, at the same time, something else entirely was compelling him to do nothing. He remained standing at the window, looking outward, covered from head to foot in a very sordid sense of shame. Looking down to the street, he saw a black cab pull up slowly onto the kerb directly below the flat – he saw the driver switch off the engine and slowly step out of the car to stretch his arms. After a few moments, he leaned into the open window of the driver's seat and pressed down on the horn, which emitted a long continuous drone that lasted for several seconds. He heard the leather of the sofa creak as she stood up, and the metallic rattle of keys being dropped onto the wooden coffee table.

'That's me. I have to go.'

'I know.'

'There must be one thing…just one thing that you want to say to me.' She said. Her voice was weak and choked up. She could barely articulate the words.

'It…' He started to say, as his hands began to shake violently. He hurriedly thrust them into his pocket, and dug his fingernails into his palms.

'Just…please just come and hold me.' She said, with exasperation in her voice.

'I'm sorry', he replied, 'I don't think I can even turn around.'

Another long and sonorous wail of the horn rung out through the room, followed by an equally long silence. A few moments later, he heard her quietly collecting the last of her belongings and walk into the hallway – and then, the barely distinguishable sound of the front door closing with a pathetic click. He turned around swiftly, and started pacing around the room, grabbing at chunks of his long hair and pulling at them. There were no more cigarettes left. His phone was buzzing and flashing on the table, and he stared resolutely at it for some time – willing it to stop… which it eventually did. He picked it up and placed it into the pocket of his trousers. He began to move quickly around the flat, marching from room to room, picking up objects without purpose, and throwing them down violently – he was finding it difficult to breathe, the arrhythmic beating of his heart was causing him pain, his stomach felt swollen, and he could feel the cold wet sensation of sweat forming on his forehead. He walked into the bathroom and opened up the mirrored cabinet above the sink. He took two oval shaped pink pills out of a blister pack and began chewing them, gathering water from the open tap with a trembling hand into his mouth in order to get rid of the powerful bitterness. After he had closed the cabinet, all at once he caught sight of his reflection and was startled. He seemed to be shaking uncontrollably; his eyes were bloodshot and convulsive, almost jumping out of his skull – the pupils were fully dilated. Almost involuntarily, he raised his right hand to his face and slapped himself with great force across the cheek and stormed out of the bathroom. He walked around the hallway, almost in circles, kicking his feet. But he was aware that it was already too late. The panic had already descended, and was running feral among his thoughts. He fell back into the wall and crumpled onto the floor hyperventilating, his vision grew dark and though he felt himself losing control of his limbs he was still very much conscious – his thoughts, expanding and expanding, in a centrifugal force, deformed and magnified with each successive revolutionary terror. He placed his hands over his eyes and attempted to weep. It was a few minutes until he came to, until his breathing had slowed down and his vision returned to normal. As he felt the Xanax kicking in, his back muscles began to relax, and the painful tension around his head began to alleviate. He pulled himself up onto his feet with some difficulty, and made his way, almost crawling, into the bedroom. In this room, which too was bare and wholly unfamiliar, the bed was unmade and without covers – and the air was stagnant and constricting. He looked around aimlessly for something to focus his attention, eventually settling on the book which lay on his bedside table, the spine broken to hold the pages open. He picked up the book of poems with his still trembling hand, and lay down onto the bed. Her scent was still on the pillow. He buried his head into it, and inhaled deeply – drinking in every last remnant. This had a calming effect on him, and he began inattentively turning and scanning the pages. He eventually focused on a certain stanza which he had highlighted in pencil with three circles and, in addition, had drawn a small cross on the right hand side. It was slightly puzzling, as he didn't remember circling this stanza, and this particular symbol meant nothing, even in his highly idiosyncratic system of annotations and marginalia which, though haphazard, generally tended to follow a particular logic. He began to suspect someone else's hand. He stared at the page for some time, reading the stanza several times through, but at first couldn't manage to take anything in. After a number of attempts, the words became clearer:

> With the heart's blood I gladden the road,
> and flowering it sticks to the dusty tunic.
> The sun, like Salomé,
> will dance a thousand times around the earth, the Baptist's head.

The image of Salomé, faceless, performing that ghastly dance, in the foreground of the freshly decapitated head of The Baptist upon the platter, played repeatedly as he began to feel drowsy and felt himself drifting off. Just as he was about to fall asleep, he felt the phone vibrate and ring in his pocket. At first he tried to ignore it, attempting to grab hold of that single elusive image which he had, only a moment before, almost captured and sublimated in some form. But it was useless. The dancer now had a face, and it belonged to her. Her dancing, as ever, was clumsy and self-consciously ironic – she smiles all too knowingly and all around her were many others; laughing with encouragement and disdain. The phone rang again, and this time he reached down into his pocket and pulled it out.

'Yes mate'

'Awrite, I tried calling earlier.'

'Never looked at my phone. What's up?'

'I'm sitting in the pub.'

'Good stuff.'

'Errr...you're supposed to be here.'

'Shit.'

'Yeah.'

'Alright, give me 15.'

It was with a concerted effort that he managed to lift himself up from the bed. First he took his left leg, which was nearest to the end of the bed but seemingly incapable of moving too much, and shoved it with his right hand so it fell onto the floor...the shock of the impact had awoken the leg somewhat, and, placing his left foot flat onto the ground – he swung his right in the same direction. He immediately regretted this decision. The force of the movement, which was overzealous and misjudged, dragged the rest of his body straight onto the floor where he fell onto his left elbow, and knocked his head off the bedside cabinet. Fortunately, it was just a small knock – and the sharp pain also had the effect of jolting his body into action. Rubbing his head, he started pulling off his t-shirt and trousers, and then walked naked through the hallway into the bathroom, where he turned on the shower. The water was too cold and he cowered as he attempted to wash his skin. As he was rubbing shower gel into his armpits, he felt two lumps. He had felt the first lump a few days back – but now there were two and, despite the brisk cold of the shower, they felt slightly warm to the touch. A momentary panic followed, but it was soon suppressed and forgotten after he had turned off the shower and made his way once more, naked, into the bedroom. He got dressed in the same clothes, and wandered around the flat for close to ten minutes while looking for his wallet and keys. The keys, as it turned out, were in his pocket. The wallet was on the bedside cabinet, underneath the book. He picked up the book, a thin paperback, and his wallet. There was no cash in the wallet. He went into the kitchen and picked up the white envelope on the table marked 'bills' with black felt tip pen, and pulled out its contents. There was £80 in cash, all stiff new notes, and a handwritten letter. He thrust the cash into his pocket, and placed the letter back into the envelope – which he threw back onto the table. After he had pocketed the remaining pills from the bathroom, he grabbed his jacket from the coat stand in the hallway and slammed the front door as he left.

The sun had vanished by the time he found himself on the street, leaving only a formless glow on the now grey and darkened sky which hinted at its former presence. After he had bought some tobacco and rolling papers in the corner shop, he crossed Sauchiehall Street, and headed towards the pub on the corner of Argyle Street. Once he was outside, he hesitated for a couple of minutes – looking around the street, startled and edgy, as if fully expecting something untoward to happen. He hurriedly rolled and lit a cigarette, taking three drags before flicking it into the battered bucket beside the door. Including the bartender, there were three people inside. One of them was his friend, the other was a man of around sixty years old wearing a Panama hat, with long sandy white hair, dressed in a beige flannel blazer, with a black Labrador asleep at his feet. The football was on. His friend sat at a table to the left of the entrance, reading the newspaper. He went to the bar and ordered a half and half, and sat down. The pub still maintained its charm – which lay in its lack thereof, and its yearly depleting collection of old scoundrels – despite what was occurring with increasing rapidity in the environs. This was why they liked it, though they'd be embarrassed to admit this. They'd been coming here for years, but were never treated as regulars – nor with anything other than suspicion. This suspicion was warranted, because despite their origins – the taint of an education is indelible, and manifests itself in all manner of involuntary affectations that no amount of dissimulation can conceal – not even from oneself. This was evident in the way they spoke to each other. His friend looked up briefly and nodded, before looking back down at his paper. He was looking at the football results.

'There he is…*El hombre invisible*.'

'Awrite.'

'How's it going?'

'Yeah, not too good mate.'

'What's happening?'

'We broke up. She just left an hour ago. She's moving down tae London.'

'Well….shit. When did that happen?'

'Suppose it started two weeks ago when she got offered the job.'

'Did she tell ye she applied?'

'No.'

'She must have been planning it then.'

'Seemed tae come fae naewhere. Do you think she could have?'

'Dunno. Probably….but suppose it won't make you feel any better tae think about it.'

'Then why'd ye mention it?'

'Shouldn't have, really.'

'I know you didn't like her.'

'Was it obvious?'

'She didn't like you either. I could see that.'

'I've reconciled myself with that fact that several people dislike me. It's a fair trade-off, since I actively dislike hunners a cunts.'

'...'

'Well?'

'What?'

'Do you want to talk about it or something?'

'Not particularly.'

'How long's that been then?'

'Three years.'

'Shit...that's a long time.'

'I canny remember any of it.'

'Surely that's not a good sign?'

'Suppose it's not.'

'What did she say exactly?'

'That I've become complacent in my affection.'

'That's what she said?'

'That was the implication.'

'Well?'

'What?'

'Does she have a point?'

'Aye.'

'Then I suppose it's all for the best.'

'Not so sure.'

'How's that?'

'Because I still love her.'

'Don't really see how that's possible, chief.'

'Just because I was bored, it doesn't mean that I didn't love her. I do in some way. I don't see how I can simply forget completely that I'm in love with her.'

'You canny forget that you were in love with her, it's true. But nonetheless, you're no longer in love with her.'

'Ok, say that you're right. Then how come I feel so utterly miserable?'

'I think you know that's only temporary.'

'Not so sure.'

'Last time I saw you was a few weeks ago, when we went tae that party. I remember talking to you and finking that you seemed so completely uninterested in anything any cunt had to say.'

'Was a pretty boring party, inntit.'

'It was…but hoachin wi fanny, as I seem to recall.'

'Dunno…don't remember.'

'Aye, it was boring…fair enough…but it wasn't just that.'

'Well?'

'What?'

'What was it then?'

'You had a look of boredom, right, and it was bordering on contempt – dunno how else tae describe it. But you were polite and had conversations with folk, listened, or pretended to listen, to what they had to say.'

'Suppose I knew what was coming.'

'Hmmm…but it's obvious.'

'What is?'

'That you no longer drew any inspiration from it.'

'I don't understand.'

'You haven't really done any work in the past few months, and before that – all you came up with was some half-arsed ideas. You do yer shifts in the bar, and do those two days in that fucking film archive or whatever. Maybe you even convince yourself that you're working, but you havenay done anything in a long time. What happened tae yer idea?'

'The idea? It's still there.'

'It's been almost four years since you came up wi that idea, and since then you've filmed a few shots and scenes, and made a few changes to the concept but aside from that: nothing. Just look at it this way, you can do more work now.'

'I suppose I can.'

'How old are you now, 28?'

'29.'

'Well?'

'What?'

'Isn't it about time that you did something?'

'I'm working on it, aye. And how about you? You're a year older than me. Still no got tae where you wanna go, have you?'

'Don't compare yourself tae me, mate. I've my own litany of unhappiness and heartbreak, and I suffered for a long time. But I always worked.'

'Well, then it's obvious that I canny work like you do.'

'How's that?'

'Dunno. I suppose I don't have the discipline, or the talent.'

'What's talent? Every cunt has talent. This world wasn't built by men with talent.'

'Aye, but the world was built a long time ago mate, its already deep in decay.'

'Fine but what am saying is, it's no just about talent – it's about work. Why can't you work?'

'Dunno.'

'You do, come on. You have an idea, you've conceptualised it well – you spent some years studying, and you've developed an aesthetic sense. Course, you don't have a surplus of resources. But you're still relatively young, you aren't starving, your job isn't particularly strenuous – and as far as I can see you're in ok health. There's really nothing preventing you from working.'

'...'

'Well?'

'What?'

'I think you know exactly what's holding you back.'

'You think it was her?'

'In a sense.'

'In what sense?'

'I don't think you really need me tae make it any clearer than that.'

'Really? Because that's pretty fucking vague isn't it?'

'Ok...let's talk about something else.'

'Fine'

'What's happening wi the flat?'

'I'm gonnae have to move out...I won't be able to afford it on ma oan.'

'Well I can move in...my lease runs out in two weeks. Could do with saving money on the rent, I'm pretty skint at the moment to be honest.'

'You think that's a good idea?'

'Why you saying that?'

'It's been a few years, and I don't have fond memories of the last time we lived together.'

'Well, whatever. It'll be different this time I suppose. At the very least you won't have to move.'

'Ok...fine. Move in whenever. Fuck sake...I feel like I'm moving backwards here.'

'Maybe it was never actually meant to move forwards, and it's actually been moving backwards all along.'

'That's pretty depressing, mate.'

'Not just you, I mean – all of it, and every cunt.'

'So…what were you getting at before?'

'What?'

'Fuck sake man…what we were just talking about before – what else?'

'Right, simmer down. There's no point talking about it. You know already.'

'What?'

'Come on, you know.'

'I really don't.'

'When did we meet?'

'It must have been almost ten years ago now.'

'Shit.'

'Yeah.'

'So, within this time – how many women have you been with?'

'I dunno.'

'Involved with?'

'Four.'

'And those were all long term relationships?'

'Aye.'

'You were in love with these women.'

'I'm still in love with them. In love with them all, in fact.'

'Well, that's just no true.'

'It's the only way that I can explain how I feel about them.'

'Yet, despite the fact that you were in love with them – each of these relationships seemed to somehow run their course, run out of momentum – leading to a sad but gentle parting of ways, without ill feeling or bitterness. See…you claim to be in love with them, but if these feelings were so intense, then I would say…you would have done more to hold onto what you had.'

'Don't think things are always that simple, mate.'

'Aye, I can imagine if it were up to you – you would have remained in those relationships out of a sense of duty to your initial feelings. But each of these women decided to leave you, in fact.... but at the same time, you never really did anything to convince them to stay.'

'Are you saying that my feelings wernay genuine?'

'Not at all, no. Each time, I saw how hurt you were and as far I could tell it was genuine. I would see you just as you are now, and for a few months you would drink more, and walk around dejectedly like some sorta wounded animal or something, with like a mournful look in your eyes. And you'd generally be an insufferable cunt. You'd entertain grand notions of flight, and conceive of some fucking huge projects that you'd lose interest in entirely a few weeks later. And eventually, you would meet someone else. And then you'd dae some work, and produce things – and, again, become insufferable in parading around your temporary happiness. You'd become drunk on it, and make that mistake that every cunt that's drunk tends to make, that is, assuming that others are as drunk as you are. Then, in a year, or two, or three, although the circumstances, incidents, or turmoils were never exactly identical, the end result was always the same.'

'Right, bit weird mate. You seemtae have given this a lot of thought.'

'No really....I'm only just seeing it now.'

'Well?'

'What?'

'What's my problem?'

'I mean…you don't have a problem....it's a fairly commonplace thing, inntit.'

'There's no point in trying tae be diplomatic now, dickhead. Just spit it out.'

'I think that you're searching for something – and you can't seem to reconcile yourself to the fact that even if it exists, then it's at best temporary. You're searching for the sublime.'

'Right...but what I'm searching for is hardly any different to what others are searching for.'

'No, you're right. And I'd go as far as tae say that it's completely identical. But you have this, let's say, constitution which makes it far more central to your everyday life than it may be for other cunts. And you don't seem tae be able to function without it.'

'You trying tae insult me?'

'Course not. Simmer down. But....what you don't seemtae realise is that there is no sustained inspiration that comes from love, or sex. To think like this is to think like a fucking idiot. Worse than a fool. A self-deluded roaster, struggling tae keep pace wi the general run. You always said, right, that you no longer hold any hope for universal salvation, and are concerned only with your own instincts and impulses and nothing more. I would say to you this then: what exactly is it that you need to work?'

'A great many things.'

'Nurturing, love, and sex. Those are your needs, which are no exactly paltry. The conclusion is inevitably the same. Your flesh is weak.'

'My flesh is weak?'

'Aye.'

'Good one.'

'Cheers.'

'Hardly original, is it?'

'It doesn't need to be original, for it to be true.'

'If you're trying tae tell me that you're completely free of desire, then that's completely fucking absurd. You have desire too, in all of the same forms that I have it – and some arbitrary judgement on my spiritual character only reflects back ontae yersel. Besides, I have no interest in the notion of spirit.'

'Neither do I. What I'm saying is that a conception of an individual spiritual essence is completely unnecessary to comprehend what this problem is. Desire is not like a metaphysical force; it's a material force, which only pretends to spiritual affectations. Its causes are material, and its effects are too. But you don't see it that way.'

'Aye yer amateur philosophy disnae really change anything here, chief.'

'Alright, alright. All I'm trying to say is this: you may have no interest in the notion of spirit, but you are nonetheless mired in it, as we all are.'

'Right.... ah see what you're accusing me of here.'

'What?'

'Romanticism.'

'And?'

'Then I would say that the idea that one can be completely free from romanticism is impossible. You're guilty of the same thing. I mean, yer a fucking painter. I mean, nae cunt paints anymore – unless they have a certain temperament.'

'No gonnae disagree, to be fair. But I wasn't accusing you of romanticism as if it were some sort of weakness to be expunged from your consciousness. It's valuable, if it can be controlled. It'd be impossible to work without it. Problem is…you can't.'

'But I have no illusions of romanticism.'

'Well, then maybe it's just you – the way that you're wired. Yeah, I've got desires as well – which are often frustrated, and longings, and lusts, and other such things…but I don't feel the sense of lack like you do. I haven't been in a relationship in the last four years. For a great many people, the fear of being alone is more profound than the fear of being dissatisfied. I may be alone, but it disnae really pain me too much to be in this state.'

'You think I'm afraid of being alone?'

'Pffft, nah. That'd be a too easy a way tae describe it.'

'Well, ok. Let's just stop fucking around here. Why don't you just tell me what you actually mean?'

'Ok then. Why do you find it so hard to be honest with yourself? If you're really serious about changing the way you live, then the only way that you can do this is to purge all traces of romanticism from your sensibilities – that way you'll know if that was the impediment all along. You still harbour some desire to be happy. But the idea of happiness won't ever really exist for someone such as yerself – you're far too sensitive to the world of sensations and things which are ultimately incompatible with happiness. Happiness requires a degree of insularity and ignorance which you've never really possessed, and never will. Clearly it hasnay served you very well. It worked for me. I harbour no illusions now. And after a period of adjusting to the sheer weight of uncompromising cynicism, it begins to feel comfortable. It allows you tae work. I say that's all you really should want, if you consider yourself an artist. But, I think it's prolly impossible for you. I don't think that it's something you're even capable of it.'

'Well?'

'What?'

'I don't know whether to feel insulted or not.'

'There's no need tae be insulted, it's my just my opinion on the matter. There's every chance that I might be wrong.'

'Suppose you're right then?'

'Has happened a coupla times.'

'Then how would I go about this? How is it even possible to step outside of an all-encompassing sensibility?'

'The easiest way, I imagine, is to shut yourself off from others. These tendencies don't thrive in solitude, in fact, they're almost entirely absent. It's hardly necessary to turn the minutiae of your everyday life intae sum form of heroic narrative when those things become so commonplace and tedious that you hardly devote any attention to them whatsoever.'

'It's hardly practical for me tae dae that, as much as I'd like to. Believe me – if it were up tae me – I wouldn't even go outside. Unfortunately, I havtae earn a living.'

'This is the problem.'

'Well?'

'What?'

'Surely there must be another way?'

'Course. Just stay away fae women. Put them outta yer mind. Avoid catching their gaze, avoid stealing glances at them, lusting after them, or talking to them if you can. And masturbate regularly in a non-committal, business-like way.'

'Right, again, seems like you given this some thought.'

'Aye, whatever…we're not talking about me here. But to be honest, as I said, I think it's impossible for you. Need at least two months. Ah think, especially in yer current state, the stench a despair sweating fae every pore, with the wounds still fresh – you'll barely last a week.'

'Maybe I should try, at least.'

'Couldn't hurt.'

'I'll think about it.'

…

A not altogether unpleasant chemical smell still clung to the air as he walked around the tables to collect empty glasses. Most of those who had been watching the performance now had shuffled off towards the bar next door, and they stood around talking to each other in false reverential tones. It was a strange odour, at first oppressive, even painful in its sharpness, yet at the same time somehow beguiling and oddly comforting. He still felt a little uneasy at what he had just witnessed. A young women, dressed in a black smock which hung over a small, slight frame, had stood on the darkened stage with a single spotlight illuminating her face. Aside from bright red lipstick there was no makeup, and though it was almost impossible to discern her exact features, he had somehow already decided that she was beautiful. Nothing was said as the spotlight dimmed and an uneasy silence descended. The stage was so dark that it was difficult to make out any more than that diminutive silhouette. After about two minutes of silence, she brought her hands up to her face. She began rubbing a red powder onto her cheeks, which illuminated the stage in short vicious flashes of chemical light; all of the variegated sensations of this process (the popping noise and apparent crackling of skin, accompanied by that bewildering smell) were driving him into one of his panics. He wanted nothing more than to run onto the stage and force her to stop. At the end of those two torturous minutes, she collapsed in a heap onto the floor...then rose swiftly and walked calmly off the stage. It was true, of course, that he was used to seeing many such occurrences, as he usually served behind the bar in the main performance space for the three days a week that he worked there. What he had intended to be a temporary job had become, after they had cut his hours at the Film Archive – if not exactly permanent – the main source of his meagre income. It paid a reasonable wage, never got too busy, and he was able to be home by midnight on most of the nights that he worked. As a keen observer and eavesdropper into the affairs of his clientele, he was able to come to certain conclusions which, though undoubtedly little more than supposition, were enough to instil in him a certain amount of resentment towards this tightly knit group of those that considered themselves to be artists, and the others who were more than happy to give their assent. A certain degree of self-conscious charlatanism pervaded all of their gestures and interactions, was all too apparent within the familiar lexicon of their aesthetic attitudes; attitudes which had seemingly become no more than a product of an undisguised dirigisme. It was, in another sense, an accord, an agreement to which all parties had decided to become complicit; the motive being their very survival. And such high stakes tend to make gamblers of us all. But there was something quite different about this particular performance. The mere fact that it had elicited any kind of response from him, never mind one so visceral and unsettling, was enough to make him believe that it had some value. There was however something else that affected his critical judgement, something, which, in the end, was all together more predictable.

It was almost closing time, and the bar in the main performance area was completely empty. He stood about listlessly, half-heartedly attempting to clean a stubborn smudge from a blue marbled pitcher. He poured himself a glass of the cheapest whiskey. The black curtain on the stage twitched slightly, until it was parted in the middle, and there emerged from behind a girl, short, with a small frame, the hood of her grey sweatshirt pulled up and obscuring her face; she held a large maroon rucksack and a towel in her hands. She walked up to the bar and sat down on one of the stools opposite him, pulling down her hood. Her mouth was large in proportion to the rest of her face, but complemented her other features – large dark green eyes, and a small almost mouse-like face. Her hair was wet, and the skin shone ever so slightly against the dim light emanating from the bar. She gathered up her still damp hair and tied it efficiently behind her head in a bun.

'Are you still serving?' She asked with an uncommonly radiant smile.

Her smile was, whatever way one looked at it, quite impressive. Neither too forced nor too lacklustre, the delicate curling of her still red lips around the corners of the mouth revealed just the right amount of her slightly crooked teeth – of which there were, inevitably, too many. It was a smile which some men would be prepared to wait an age to be able to witness, yet was offered without the slightest hesitation – and with far too much enthusiasm – for what was an ordinary question to a stranger. The effect on him was palpable, and he was momentarily taken aback.

'No...it's fine, I can get you something.'

'Oh, good.'

'What would you like?'

'Could I have a gin and tonic?'

'Of course.'

He picked up a glass tumbler from under the bar and filled it with ice, but as he turned around to reach for the bottle of gin on the middle shelf, his hand began to tremble and, slightly flustered, he attempted to subtly glance over his shoulder. Fortunately, she wasn't paying attention. Her brow was furrowed, and she seemed to be immersed in a book that she had pulled out of her bag. From the same bag, she pulled out a packet of long thin cigarettes and teased one into her mouth using her teeth. She was on the point of lighting up, when he placed the drink in front of her.

'I'm sorry, you can't smoke here.'

'Oh...but there's no one around, right?' She asked, smiling once more.

'Ok...wait a second.'

He dashed out from behind the bar and ran to the front door excitedly, fumbling the keys from his pocket, which dropped onto the floor. He hurriedly picked them up, and closed the three locks on the main door in a rapid, fluid, motion and then walked back towards the bar nonchalantly.

'...but you have to give me one too.' He said.

She lit the cigarette with a determined gesture and took a long deliberate drag, before offering it to him. There was a slight wet red smudge on the tip, which tasted sweet as he placed it to his lips.

'You look like you really needed that.' She said, without taking her eyes from the page.'

'I'm trying to quit. It's been a week.'

She suddenly looked up at him, and screwed up her face. 'Oh… that's so sad. Why would you do that? It obviously gives you pleasure.'

'Well….I suppose, some things have happened recently that have made me more painfully aware of mortality.'

She kept staring at him, without saying anything or blinking. Her face had assumed an overly serious aspect, and she seemed to be looking him up and down.

'Are you sick?' She asked.

'No, I'm fine.'

'But you're suddenly afraid to die….that's worrying.'

'I don't think I'm afraid to die. I'm not sick either. At least, if I am – then I'm certainly not aware of it. I just feel…unwell.'

'Then maybe you should go to the doctor.' She said, with a smile.

'It's more of a spiritual malaise.'

'Oh dear, that isn't good is it?'

'No, I suppose not.'

'You're very serious aren't you?'

'Not really…I'm just unhappy, I guess.'

'Well....think about it this way.' She began, as she stubbed the end of her cigarette into the ashtray, and placed another one into her mouth, 'You shouldn't ignore the things that give you pleasure, just because other things make you unhappy. Because it's pleasure that regulates your life, and stops you from dying miserable.'

'Ok…that seems like a slightly narcissistic way to view the world.'

'Why do you say that?'

'I really liked your performance.' He replied, noticing his misstep and changing tack. She suddenly became broody, and looked down towards her book.

'Thanks.' She replied.

'Have you done this piece before?'

'No. This is the first time.'

'Well....'

'I don't really like to talk about my work. Not now. I'd rather not, if that's ok?'

'Well…yeah. Anything I'd say would be probably be irrelevant anyway.'

'Do you have a very low opinion of yourself?'

'Why do you ask that?'

He detected a slight hint of condescension in her question and the accompanying gesture. She was still smiling, and in fact he had begun to suspect that she couldn't do otherwise in social interactions. But it had become deformed somehow – somehow crooked, a smirk, followed by a laugh.

'You seem offended, I didn't mean it like that.'

'Like what?' He asked, so bluntly that he even surprised himself.

'Well, you've turned all defensive for some reason.'

'I'm sorry, I just don't really know how to respond.'

'Well, it wasn't a loaded question.'

'Do you want me to answer truthfully?'

'Hhmmm…I guess? But that would be dangerous wouldn't it?'

'Well, the problem is that I don't have a low opinion of myself... if anything I have an inflated sense of my own self-worth – and probably an overestimation of my talents, which are at odds with my actual circumstances.'

'How come?'

'I work in a bar.'

'Do you?'

'Yes.'

'Oh come on, as if your shite job means anything. Everyone has a shitty job. I have a shitty job. You must do something else, if you think that you have talents.'

'I make films.'

'Oh dear...'

'Is there something wrong with that?'

'What kind of films do you make?'

'...'

'Don't you want to tell me?'

'I wouldn't know how to begin to describe what I want to do. Because if I did, I'll hear the words coming out and they'll start to feel prosaic, and I'll be disgusted with myself.'

'Oh...it's totally, like, abstract then?' She said with a mischievous grin, taking a drink of her gin.

She placed a finger into the glass and fished out one of the three half melted ice cubes, put it into her mouth, and began chewing it noisily.

'Let me see your hands', she asked suddenly, the remnants of the ice cube still rattling against her teeth. He held them up awkwardly.

'No, bring them over here.'

He walked slowly towards the bar and held out his hands with the palms facing upward. He tried to catch her eye, but she had already ducked below the bar, and was rummaging around in the open bag at her feet.

'Yeah, that's what I thought.' She said as she remerged, looking down at them while screwing up her face slightly. She had a white plastic tube in her hand.

'They look a wee bit dry, you really need to moisturise them. Here, hold them out.'

She squeezed two large blobs of viscous white liquid onto each palm, and began gently rubbing the moisturiser into each hand carefully whilst humming a song to herself. The song sounded familiar.

'There' she said as she finished. 'You should always take extra care of your hands.'

'Why?'

'Why? Because you have very nice hands, they're very long and elegant. I envy people with beautiful hands. Mine are small and stubby.'

'I think they're very sweet.'

'Oh thank you…I suppose we see other people's hands differently from our own.'

'Why don't you want to talk about your work?'

'Talking about why I don't want to talk about my work, would be talking about my work – wouldn't it?'

'I don't think it would.'

He poured himself another whiskey, then grabbed the bottle of gin from the counter and waved it at her. She nodded her head coyly.

'But…you didn't talk about your work – so why should I?'

'But at least I explained why I didn't want to.'

'Erm, so did I? But I can't figure out whether you're interested or you're just being nosey?'

'Doesn't really matter.'

'What difference would it make if I talked about it? You saw it, and you responded to it. If I told you how I came up with the idea, or what I feel about it – or what I was thinking when I was performing: it would be pointless. You'll either see my perspective or you won't. Either way you'll feel differently about it than you did before, and maybe you'll even begin to hate it.'

'There's no way around that though, you're going to have to explain it somehow – to someone, eventually. You'll be forced to explain it, unless you're satisfied with conjecture – with misrepresentation. And I don't think I would be comfortable with that.'

'Hhmmm….maybe that's because you have such an inflated opinion of yourself?'

'Maybe.'

'Ok. All I can tell you is that when I perform, I return into a state of harmony – where everything which usually makes up my personality is irrelevant, where it's alien. I can push myself in any direction, I can transform my body into something which is alien to myself – and that is the only thing which comes close to freedom for me. So, if I can attain this state – this blissful state of being – then what do I care what comes from this? Explaining where it comes from would only complicate things.'

II

SWARMING MICROBIAL SUPERSTITIONS

The bed creaked as he sat upright and reached for his phone on the bedside table. The phone was dead and it was morning. As the heavy curtains were closed, the room was still dark as he fumbled around to switch on the small bedside lamp. The light was much brighter than anticipated, and revealed all of the darkened corners of that unfamiliar space in which he, at that point, found himself. His head was throbbing, and there was an empty pulling at his stomach – the room, cold, unwelcoming and of medium size, was on the third floor of a yellow sandstone tenement – the walls had been painted white, the ceilings were high with cornicing around the edges. The bed was in the middle of the room against one wall and facing another, large, white wall which spanned the entire length of the room; the wall was bare but for a lone rectangular mirror, slightly dusty, and three solid coloured silk scarves (one yellow, one red, and the other a light blue) which were pinned, seemingly at random, and with no desire to perform a decorative function, to different parts of the wall. To the right hand-side of the bed, there were two large windows; and to the left – a long white clothes rail with various dresses. On the bedside table there was a makeup box, a selection of different medications in blister packs, and a single book: *The Anthropology of Ritual* by Professor Augustus Wyndham. Beside the corner window, to the right of the bed, there was a large desk with a pile of sketches across it, a box of oil paints, a record player, and an ashtray full of cigarettes. Next to the desk, there was a small box full of vinyl, and a clunky looking music stand with a battered half-strung viola propped up against it. None of these objects and furnishings, nor their arbitrary resemblance to any human dwelling, had the effect of assuaging the feeling of acute discomfort which he suddenly felt, and the sum of all of these little details began to feel entirely monstrous and malevolent. A sharp pain struck at his temples, almost blinding his vision. As he stood up from the bed to open the curtains, the tendon of his right ankle buckled slightly and he struggled to stay on his feet – before eventually sitting down on the edge of the bed in no small amount of pain. The door closed behind him, and he heard the sound of laughter.

'I think it might be sprained. Do you remember stumbling on the stairs last night?'

'I do now.'

She stood at the door, naked, smiling and holding two mugs. She walked over and handed one over to him.

'Is it coffee?'

'Is that a problem?'

'I stopped drinking caffeine...it makes me too nervous.'

'There's no need to be nervous', she said as she kissed him lightly on the forehead. 'Don't drink it. I can make you, like, some herbal tea or something? Maybe you should eat something too... but I'm gonna take a shower now.'

'Do you live alone?'

'Do you think I'd just walk around naked if I didn't?'

'I wouldn't know. I only just met you.'

'I live alone.'

She turned, awkwardly and abruptly, and walked out of the room closing the door firmly behind her. With some difficulty he managed to stand up, limping around the side of the bed gathering the clothes that were strewn around the floor, and began dressing himself. As he pulled on his trousers, he retrieved a single pink pill wrapped in cling film from the inside folds of his battered wallet and swallowed it whole. He sat back down on the edge of the bed to tie the laces of his boots, then walked over to the mirror on the opposite wall. The bags under his eyes protruded outward, more so than normal, and the dark circles seemed somehow more pronounced; his eyes were red and bloodshot, possibly through fatigue – certainly from too much whiskey; his hair was sticking up at the back, and he attempted, unsuccessfully, to flatten it with his palm. Underneath the mirror was a faded black and white photo of a nude woman, lying down on a towel on some loch-side pebble beach. Her head was turned in the opposite direction to the camera and it was impossible to make out her face. Underneath the photo was a post-it, and there, in a flowing feminine scrawl, there was a fragment of a phrase which seemed, at once, altogether too familiar: 'You have every reason to believe that you will die, one day.' He felt suddenly light headed, walked back over to the bed and lay down. As he closed his eyes and felt himself on the verge of drifting off to sleep, a shrill metallic clang (a pipe creaking somewhere beyond the ceiling) jolted him awake. He reached over for the book on the bedside cabinet and, turning to a random page, began reading out the words in a croaking and monotonous voice: 'When the women would return from the forest, their husbands would notice the dried blood and feathers which had covered their clothing. Thinking that something terrible had occurred, they would order the women to divest themselves of their garments and perform a ritual dance to cleanse the hunting and foraging party of the evil which they had, unwittingly, brought into the camp. The dance consisted of several stages, the first of which simulated...' he heard the door close with a click. She stood in the doorway in a yellow robe, her hair bundled up in a towel, screwing up her face as she scanned the room for something. She walked over to one of the bedside cabinets and pulled a hair drier from one of the drawers.

'Where's the bathroom?' He asked, his voice still sounding hoarse and gravely.

'The last door on the right before the front door.'

He walked towards it and turned around to survey the room from the doorway; she was facing away from him, and having removed her robe, she stood naked by the window as a powerful stream of hot air from the noisy drier blew her hair around her head. Her skin was an almost translucent white and pallid, there was a slight, almost imperceptible, droop to her shoulders. The outline of her spine could be traced from the top of her shoulder blades down to the small of her back, where there was a small brown mole about the size of a ten-pence piece. He heard the door to the bedroom creak slightly behind him, and feeling something shuffle past his feet, looked down to see a slightly overweight white Persian cat saunter into the room sniffing the air derisively, turning her impetuous little face cautiously towards the unknown intruder, staring for two seconds, before turning back around, and listlessly walking towards her owner who was pulling on underwear. She bent over and picked up the cat and rubbed her nose against its face. The sight of her being affectionate to the animal made him feel almost embarrassed. As she turned around, she noticed that he was still standing there at the doorway. She stared blankly at him for a few moments, and seemed puzzled.

'This is Rosie.'
'Hello Rosie'
'Rosie doesn't like strangers.'
'I can imagine.'

'You're really scowling right now, is there a problem?'

'No, no, sorry – I just got a little distracted. Just gonnae…going to splash some water oan ma face.'

'Haha…awrite then.'

The hallway was dark and sparse with wooden flooring and little furniture – there were a few framed childhood photographs of her; a solitary little girl in a light blue playsuit standing on a grey sandy beach, gripping a red bucket and spade, seemingly on the point of tears – a rather young teenager smiling coquettishly with dark eye makeup and a nose piercing, standing in the middle of a group of friends wearing school uniforms. A photo of her in a black bodycon dress – standing in the university quadrangle under the large oak tree, gripping a red cylindrical parchment holder, whilst the wind blew her gown behind her. In the bathroom he ran the cold water tap at full blast and held his wrists underneath until they became numb, then gathered some of the frothing water in his cupped hands and splashed it over his face. It didn't have the desired effect, and if anything made him feel slightly more nauseous. As he walked back down the hallway he caught sight of her, fully dressed now, walking towards the kitchen with the mugs in her hands – the cat plodding behind her at a leisurely pace.

When he entered the kitchen, she was already busy placing bread into the toaster, and removing butter and jam from the fridge – she turned around every now and then to glance down towards the cat, who was skulking around at her feet, waiting to be fed. She took a can of tuna from the cupboard and emptied it onto a pink plastic bowl with several black paw-prints around its edges, then placed the bowl onto the floor next to the refrigerator and the litter tray. Rosie approached the bowl cautiously and, contemplating it for a few moments, sniffed at it – then proceeded to walk away disdainfully towards the bedroom. Her owner looked on forlornly, and seemed to be more than a little upset.

'She doesn't like tuna anymore, and I can't figure out why. I don't like feeding her normal cat food. Here, sit down – do you want jam or marmalade?'

'I'm not sure if I can eat anything just now, it's ok...really.'

'But I just made you toast, you have to eat something. Why does nobody want to eat anything today? It's very upsetting.'

'No, don't be upset, I'll have some toast then.'

'I'm not going to force you.'

'You're not...I'll have some toast.'

'Ok, do you want some blueberries too? Or I have some oranges and bananas too. Or I can make porridge with honey and blueberries. I like putting the blueberries and porridge in the microwave so they kind of melt, and then you put honey over them – and it's...it's just amazing.' At this point, it seemed as if she had become disconcerted, and was more hurried in her actions. She pulled two sachets of instant porridge from the cupboard into two bowls pouring almond milk into them, then noisily throwing them into the microwave for a few minutes, while she wandered around the kitchen ordering around certain minor infelicities which could never, under normal circumstances, be considered 'mess.' She threw blueberries onto each of the bowls and blasted each for around thirty seconds, burning her hand slightly as she brought them to the table and placed one in front of him with a spoon.

'There you go.' She took the spoon and dipped it into a jar of dark honey, and slowly dripped it over each bowl of porridge.

'Are you alright?' He asked.

'Yes, of course I am. Why are you asking?' She countered, smiling, having fully recovered her composure. 'Well, are you going to try it?'

He took a spoonful of the sickly sweet porridge to his mouth, and she never took her eyes off him until he had swallowed it. He smiled awkwardly and cautiously began eating more, until she seemed satisfied that he was enjoying it. She looked down at her bowl, took an amount of porridge that barely even reached beyond the tip of her spoon and brought it to her mouth before placing the spoon back down onto the table. She took a pack of cigarettes from her pocket and lit one, angling her head to the side to exhale the smoke away from him.

'Ugh, I have to work in two hours.'

'Where do you work?'

'I do one day a week in a café down the road. And in my studio, it's not far from here either. Do you always look this grumpy in the morning?'

'I think so…takes me a while to wake up I guess.'

'What are your plans today?'

'Dunno. It's Saturday and I'm hungover…I've squandered any hope of a fulfilling weekend already.'

'That's a terrible thing to say to me.'

'No that's not what I meant…I mean, if anything this has already been the high point, and I can't do anything…productive, or something. I didn't mean to say that…you know what I mean?'

'I know that you're *mean*.'

'I'm sorry…I really shouldn't talk until I've been up for at least two hours…'

'Hahaha, God, I'm only fucking with you…it's fine.'

'Good…because I think you're incredible…and I'd like to see you again, if I can.'

At this her shoulders seemed to tighten, and she sat upright in the chair – looking out towards something outside the window, perhaps at nothing in particular, for a few minutes.

47

'Sure', she finally said.

As he walked, slightly limping, out onto the street, he realised that he was in the Southside – a fact which did not seem to linger too much in his thoughts in the sybaritic night just passed, or in any case hadn't made a strong enough impression as to be noteworthy when, admittedly, he had been eight (or perhaps nine) whiskeys deep...he wandered down a leafy yet inconspicuous street – it was Shawlands or Pollokshields he could be sure of that much – it occurred to him that his phone was out of battery...they had sat drinking well into the early hours, until perhaps two, or three. The conversation was easy and responsive, its ebb and flow was seamless and fluid – it was the type of conversation which, when supplemented by the intoxicating effects of whiskey, always seemed to instil within him a buoyant and entirely artificial confidence completely at odds with his natural reserve. Indeed, it had seemed to go so well that he was scarcely able to control the situation, or (had he been so inclined) even to prevent its eventual conclusion. Sometimes, the cards just seem to fall in your favour – he thought to himself. And with this thought, an involuntary grin plastered itself over his face, and there was a spring in his step as he walked to...fuck no knows where....a main road, to get a....bus? It was around late morning and he had to meet his friend, who was moving his stuff into the flat today. The hangover, as he could now fully perceive, was of the depersonalising type – that is – one which begins with an almost pleasant feeling of unreality yet underneath, obscured by the nihilistic sensation of feeling completely unconcerned by – or unconnected to the material world, lay the promise of much corporeal unpleasantness in the hours to come. He could, as he saw it, start drinking again as a delaying tactic (it was Saturday, and that was fine), or wait it out until the inevitable gloom digs in, entrenches itself behind impenetrable fortifications until...well at least until Wednesday, nowadays. A shocking state of affairs. Still, he had cause to be happy...as much cause as any man after such a night. He felt like giving someone a high-five. No one around. They had walked around aimlessly after he closed up the bar – he walked with her to get her bike, which she had locked up on the corner of Rose Street. He sensed her unwillingness to leave. He said that she really shouldn't be cycling after drinking so much. She agreed. They're eyes locked, and they stared at each other for the prescribed amount of time before....it wasn't as intense as he expected after they got a taxi back to her flat. She put on a record and poured glasses of stale red wine that tasted like it had been open for a week...they sat on her floor and she kept grasping his hands, and stroking them gently. She spoke about many things, and smiled, and laughed, and made jokes, mentioned people they both knew in common; but at no point, he now realised, did he discover anything he could genuinely say told him something about her.... herself, her...inner life, which had a short time before seemed, by all accounts, both to external appearance and through limited insight, to be so much richer than that of others, himself included. And then they had sex. It was sensual in an almost predictable way, cautious and undemanding, languorous but not particularly time consuming. He wasn't sure that she came. He came over her face.... she asked him too. He felt a little weird about it. He had never done it before, and neither had he ever had the desire. Why had she waited so long to answer when he asked to see her again? It was not the type of question which he should have asked himself at that point. There's an almost obscene dichotomy to her body...she's perhaps a year or two older than himself, yet her mouse-like face seemed frozen in that blissful period of the first part of a women's twenties...young, in possession of a certain naiveté, innocent of wrinkled cynicism, soulful, tender and melancholic without cause....this impression continued down from the face, the neck, and chest...but ended abruptly at the hips. There, things took a salacious turn...the hips were supple and disproportionately ample, the thighs, though slight, were rounded and firm – supporting a surprisingly large arse – one which delightfully expanded when liberated from their denim constraints. He felt himself becoming hard in spite of the hangover. After some time he managed to come upon Pollokshaws Road...a light drizzle, the natural state of city, covered his face in a wet mist as he caught the Number 3 bus towards town. Nothing comparable to lying next to a soft warm body, he thought to himself. He must see her again. But how? In his temporarily broken mind, the doubt had expanded and mutated, drowning all those minute patches of hope within its viscous blackness...I am like the king of a very rainy kingdom, rich but powerless, young but grown very old. And of work, what of work? A slow but discerning work, indeed – never close to completion, yet never short of ideas. An incompetent and indolent work, never in possession of drive, never attaining an objective nor with a telos in mind...not without minor inspiration, worthy of minor artists, by whom he was surrounded, but in the desperate remnants of unsteady self-belief, never a part of: no. With music the sounds no longer came to his ears, and with words too immediate, devoid of the experience which it so desired to come in contact with, and when such contact finally came...nothing, nothing but more doubt and more ideas half formed and still-born...and of heartbreak which vanquishes the last dregs of inspiration and leaves only a wallowing somnolence. Funerals and fireworks. Then came the image, and the sound, and the word in totality – yet it progresses at nothing swifter than a long glacial pace, and time, which is brief, cares nothing for perfectionism. But that face, those eyes, and that magnificent body. Yes, nothing comparable. He'd a need a second opinion, of course.

'How long was that then?'

'Two weeks?'

'Two weeks.'

'How was it?'

'She was incredible.'

'The sex?'

'The sex? What? No, I don't know. It was fine. It was sex.'

He was thankful, at least, that there wasn't as much heavy lifting as he had dreaded on the walk home. His ankle was better, but was painful nonetheless. All of his friend's possessions were in black bags – and there were less than ten. Perhaps nine. It annoyed him that his friend had so little, but more so that he seemed intent to parade his commitment to such a self-consciously ascetic existence with adolescent glee. Of course, it worked. Some of those bags were heavy, with hard protruding edges, and others were soft and billowy – who knows what was inside? Well, it was obvious. It became obvious to him, the intended effect: that he would never be so unencumbered and weightless. As they got to the end of the pile, his friend went off to take a piss. He grabbed the last couple of bags, opened the door to the little room, and threw them hard against the wall and slammed the door shut.

He'd given him the single room which she had optimistically called the 'studio' a couple of years ago. There was never very much sign of work whenever he had wandered in to talk to her. There was a desk with some pens and some oil paints, an easel, and a bookshelf, with some magazines – she spent a lot of time in there during the last few months. He only now recalled this. He'd gone home to East Kilbride the other weekend. His Dad was sat in the living room drinking the single can of Carlsberg Special Brew he drank every evening, and listening to talk-sport: 'Canny say

I'm really that surprised tae be honest, son'. He sunk further into the new sofa, and tried to read the paper to ignore the inevitable critique. 'She was a nice girl, a wee bit up herself – but she was nice.' The sofa, new by the looks of it, probably purchased at the time of the new kitchen, and new flooring in the living room, strained under the weight of this expert opinion. His father was without imagination in most things, and in most matters never strayed too far from the middle ground, which he occupied enthusiastically and without any sense of doubt. I suppose it was through necessity. He'd left school at 16, and drove taxis all of his life. At the centre of the mantelpiece in the living room, for at least the last twenty years, there was a small wooden cross with a rosary bead wrapped around it, and next to that a small golden statue of the Gautama – the only visible manifestation of credulousness in what had mostly been a house without much interest in such things. His mother had gone to church infrequently, and she'd bring him along sometimes. He had found it boring, and having bony knees made it painful to kneel for too long. And after the day when they had buried her, 15 years ago, he hadn't had much cause to step inside one ever again. His Dad leaned forward. 'Need to get yourself a proper job, son. She was a nice girl, but I'm not really surprised – you need to give them stability.' He turned off the radio, and sat upright and rubbed his temples, giving some consideration to the problem. 'You know about cameras, what about working for the BBC?' He smiled broadly, resumed his reclined position, flicked the radio back on, and went back to his can. It was a thoroughly infuriating and depressing experience, as most exchanges with his father invariably tended to be.

Not that it mattered now. It's all in the past. Nothing comparable. In 4 weeks he would be 30 years old. Did he ever imagine that at 29, he would be such a fucking loser? He had stopped paying attention at some point, perhaps at 23, settled into a life of mediocre domesticity, a second-rate facsimile of a settled existence, with bohemian pretensions, and assumed, was so bloody sure, that the work would just come, that it would flow unhindered, perfectly formed, from this coddled little routine of mutual low-level resentment and jealousy. Didn't they always say that you have to suffer? Why had he assumed that it was possible to work without suffering? Well, he was suffering now. His 23-year-old self would look upon his current self with nothing less than utter contempt. A dark blue circle painted on a canvas, not a perfect circle by any means, with a thin white covering of oil paint; the blue is dark, an inky blue, almost black – and the white is a dirty white, a chalk like white – the texture of powder on a blackboard eraser. This was the current image. It had come to him last night. If only he could figure out what this meant, exactly, then perhaps he would be able to do some work today. First, he had to shake off this hangover. His friend, as it happened, as it was Saturday, was also hungover – so they decided, without much ceremony, and with little discussion, to go to the off-license and get a couple of cans – just to get back on an even level, back to the zero-state; drink themselves back to normal. Standard practise. Then maybe he would have a nap, get something to eat, and then get to work. He got his phone out. It was almost two. 'Just wanted to say that I had such a fun time with you last night, and I'd really like to do it again sometime.' He typed off quickly, distractedly, and sent the message without giving it a second thought. He immediately regretted the wording. They sat down, ate a bag of chips, and started drinking. The first sip of alcohol after a hangover always has a poisonous odour, but satisfies nonetheless – the second is more discreet in its effects, comforting, hiding its deleterious intent behind an affable guise of affected familiarity. They finished the first couple of cans.

'The implication, the feeling which you're supposed to feel is... what? It's a guilt, I suppose, a guilt that you've somehow become a reactionary all of sudden. I'm already guilty…I don't need to feel any more guilty than I need tae…other cunts are more guilty than me. I guess I wanted nothing more than for people to feel less afraid and to be free to be anyone they want. But it's boring now, that's ma main problem wi it. It's become boring. I mean, who really gives a shit about any of it, in the last instance? About every cunt's boring minor stories? It's a distraction. Every cunt needs to realise this. Naebody cares. That should be the final point. I don't care, not because I'm unfeeling and callous, but because ultimately it isn't interesting.'

'It isn't interesting to you, but it is to other people. But I suppose the capacity to have some sorta thrill has disappeared. The thrill that comes with defying conventions: the thrill of transgression. It just doesn't have the same effect when it's become the main conversation.' He checked his phone in between each sentence. But still nothing. She's probably working.

'Exactly. And, it isn't political – is it? It'll never really be political, it will always only be personal, because it only creates an infinitely reducible and divisible set of grievances, and then special pleading to address those grievances, and nothing is left except a collection of different groups. All anyone wants is recognition…and by who exactly? Atomisation. Division only benefits the status quo, that's why universalism, has always been the *sine qua non* of action. You heard that phrase *sine qua non*? – Ah fucking love that phrase, it's quality. Here…you know why cunts top themselves? Well…lets be real…men. You know why men kill themselves? Because they're fundamentally born for action right, but they've put it off, they've deferred it, tried to rationalise that its unnecessary, that the brutal fucking reality of the human condition has somehow changed in the past twenty years haha…they repress it…but it's always gonnae come back, and if you don't let it out, this violent energy, you'll have no choice but to turn it inward. It's a final act, a final pitiful form of action, for the all those cunts who've been unable to do anything else.'

'Yeah yeah, totally mate. Be a man of action...' He replied without really thinking. They'd already had about four cans each by this point, and, as he opened a fifth, realised in passing that he was about to leave the zero-state behind. He took out his phone again, and re-read what he had sent: 'Fun'. Was it 'fun'? Was he the type of guy that only has 'fun'? The type of guy that's only really interested in 'fun'? He wasn't that guy, he was more complex – he could be sure of that. He wanted more than that. Of course he liked fun just as much as the next guy, but he wanted more than fun from her. If she only wanted to have fun too, then she would have replied already. Of course she would have. Was it even fun? It was kind of awkward, and uncomfortable. Everything about her was incredible. But was it fun? So why the fuck did he write fun? It was offensive to her, to himself even, to describe last night as only 'fun'. No wonder she hasn't replied yet. When she writes back, he'll tell her exactly how he feels. Poetically. There was, after all, a certain poetry and pathos to their encounter – she couldn't have missed that either.

'Who you texting?'
'Nah, naebody. Girl from last night.'
'Well?'
'What?'
'What did she say?'
'Nothing, she hasn't replied.'
'Right.'
'Why hasn't she replied?'

'How am I supposed to know?'

'She's probably still at work.'

'Well, there you go.'

'But, she works in cafe – and it's a Saturday. It's almost 5. I doubt that they were so busy that she didn't have the time to check her phone.'

'Yeah, you're right. She's probably read it, and she's probably dingying you.'

'Why you saying that?'

'I didnae say that, you did. When did you send it?'

'Coupla hours ago.'

'No idea, I don't reply to texts immediately. Neither do you for that matter. What's the problem here? The only difference is you shagged her last night, and somehow that deserves a completely different attitude from her to the situation.'

'What you saying? That I'm no playing the game? What's the game?'

'I dunno, mate. Maybe you should have waited till the next day or something – then sent her something casual and borderline dismissive. That works, I found.'

'Why? What's the point in that? I mean, I really like her.'

'You really like her? What do you like about her?'

'She seems interesting.'

'What's interesting about her? She's some sorta artist, she's middle class and educated, and attractive in an unusual way. Those are basically the only reasons why this particular encounter means anything more to you than if she were unattractive, or even attractive in a more obvious way, and only worked in a cafe and nothing else. She fits into a certain aesthetic preference you have.'

'How?'

'She's an approximation tae an image of some sorta ideal you haven't been able to shake off since your adolescence. It's an expectation of what you feel you deserve – her mores, her talents, her tastes, as understood only by you. But at this point you know so little about her that's it pointless to assume that these things will be true – because the reality is certain to be far less exciting. So what's the point in even obsessing about it?'

'Come on. I described her to you. She's like no one I've ever met before. I'm sure of it. It's insulting to suggest that she's similar to every other girl who happens to be all of those things. She has real talent, real substance, real history. She has an inner life – and it's beautiful, it has to be.'

'You mean that *she* is beautiful.'

'Aye, she is. So what?'

'And if she wasn't? I daresay you wouldnae really be that fussed.'

'Maybe it's only me that finds her beautiful.'

'Doubt it, mate. I doubt you're the only cunt tae find her beautiful. And I'd go so far as tae say she's beautiful in a way that's tragic, or inspiring, or affirming, or something like that? She has an inner life, for sure, but at this point – you know nothing about it. So what you oan about? Everyone has an inner life. Most of them aren't beautiful. But almost all of us will probably go right to the end of our own lives without ever being certain exactly what the inside of another person's life is made up of. You can only guess – you can only embellish those details to suit your own fantasy. You'll never find out for sure.'

'I think you're bringing something else intae this which has nothing tae dae wi her…and actually, nothing tae dae wi me either.'

'And what's that?'

'Your problem with women.'

'Bullshit.'

'It's true. Yeah, you might say that you admire women, and you'd never ever let it be known that you think this way, but you find it hard to respect them entirely...to allow them the same level of intellectual consideration that you'd give to me, or any of our other friends who happen to be men. You don't talk to our friends who are women in the same way as you do with men – I've seen it myself, all the time. Occasionally, you might indulge in conversations with them about things which you believe matter, but it's never really a conversation – it's always light-hearted, never engaged, never authentic – it's only ever frivolous.'

'That's nonsense.' He replied, a little bit aggrieved, 'I was pretty much raised by women. I've known far more women who are more talented and a lot more intelligent than I could ever be. So I don't really see why you're saying that.'

'It really costs nothing to say those things. You're stupid, women are intelligent; you're talentless, women are brilliant...but you'll only ever say these things when the ways in which they are talented or intelligent don't fundamentally interest you, or doesn't threaten your own interests – when they don't tread on your turf. As long as they're having different conversations from you, it's easy enough to give them empty praise and carry on.'

'And how's that any different from you?'

He wasn't entirely invested in the conversation, potentially acrimonious as it had become, and realised that he was simply escalating the situation needlessly. Besides, they were fairly drunk at this point – and now the alcohol had run out. He looked around the living room. In the two weeks since she had left, the condition of the flat had deteriorated markedly. Unwashed plates and mugs were dotted around the floor, dirty t-shirts were thrown haphazardly over the furniture, there were spots of cigarette ash on the carpet, the sink was filled with unwashed dishes – a pungent stench of mould and cigarette smoke clung stubbornly to the air. He wasn't, by nature, particularly messy – or at least, having undergone prolonged periods of enforced conditioning, he hadn't been for the last few years. Something had given way two weeks ago – the inevitable return of the repressed. He now felt almost duty-bound to make his living conditions as squalid as possible, and in truth it had the counterintuitive effect of soothing his temperament, of lessening the ever present state of unease which he lived under. The lumps under his armpit began to throb a little. 'Do' it again sometime. Did he really write that? Do it. Yes, he just wants to 'do' it all the time, so he'd like to 'do' her again. This is probably what she thinks. Hang out, spend time, do something – but just 'do it'? She isn't going to reply.

'This place is a fucking midden by the way.'

'Yeah, I know. Whatever.'

There was a short sharp burst of rain when they left the pub and they were soaked, but just managed to catch the off-license before it closed. He couldn't really walk straight at this point, and gripped the plastic bag full of beer and a little quarter bottle of whiskey to his chest in a protective embrace. The weekend was a write off, now. They were headed to a party on the other side of the park. Still no answer – he would stop hoping at this point. Of course, he still checked his phone periodically. Not entirely impossible that something might have happened. Nothing too tragic, nothing too harmful or distressing. Things happen, more often than not. It was definitely sent. It was definitely read. The mystery which was once attached to that formerly elusive and troubling question had forever been silenced by the banal progress of insipid technology. He would never be able to adapt to this paradigm. The hope of technology, that is, the very notion of the future, of a future, had ceased to exist for him with the realisation that it cares nothing for subtlety – that it would be nothing more than a democratised clawing familiarity, a maladroitly inflicted lexicon of crassness, a standardised narrative of cheap fiction and imperious narcissism. They were walking right through the middle of the unlit park, and the moon was visible just above the University tower, its glow imperceptible and unwelcoming, providing little illumination onto the path. It's difficult not to feel personally offended, he thought to himself. As a man who is highly sensitive, with easily hurt feelings: it's considerably more difficult. He wondered if he had ever been so callous to other women. Well...probably. But if a man is adrift at sea, utterly weak and spent from calling out for help for days, his voice completely exhausted, with the last reserves of energy he possesses, reaches out one last time to grasp at something he sees in front of him before he loses consciousness to merge forever with the growing darkness which surrounds him – you would reach a hand towards him. You would help him out of the water. Perhaps when he's safely on the boat, wrapped in a foil sheet and taking meek little sips of hot tea – you could sit at his side, smile, maybe give him a wee pat on the head – have a quiet word with him and say: 'Sorry, I'm not really interested'. What had he ever done that was so bad, to be treated with such cruelty? He was being pathetic, he knew it. What did it matter? He'd been alone for all of two weeks, and there he was – willing himself to fall in love with the first warm body to rub up against him. It was pathetic, no doubt about that. What did he really have to gain from this, what would it lead to? He didn't even remember what it felt like, fucking her. It certainly wouldn't lead to work, which is the only thing that matters now. They approached the dilapidated tenement where the party was already starting; the sound of an amplifier being switched on could be heard, and a few notes were hit on a synthesiser. There was a dead rat outside the building door which was held ajar by a milk crate, a low resonant hum came from the broken buzzer. They went up two flights of stairs to the entrance of the flat, where there was a little wooden table. A severe looking girl with a peroxide blonde bowl cut and a septum piercing, sat behind the table with a black marker pen, charging entrance. His friend dug around in his pockets and pulled out a fistful of coins and looked at them forlornly.

'How much?'
'Three'
'That's all I've got.'
'You don't have three pounds?'
'It's probably like two.'
'It's for the band, for their petrol.'
'Nah, sorry. Can you let me in?'
'Dunno.'
'Well…I have to say…that's quite niggardly.'
'Sorry, what?'
'I said you're being niggardly.' He replied, with a stupid smile.
'What the fuck is that supposed to mean?'
'What do you think it means?'
'Well, it's pretty fucking offensive. How can you say something like that?'

He pulled his wallet out and took out a fiver and handed it to the girl, pulling his friend aside a little as he did so: 'It actually just means tight', he interjected with surprising eloquence.

'Right…so he's just being a dick then?' She replied, allowing herself to smile briefly.

'Ha! Different etymology entirely. Interesting how you assumed though, isn't it? Isn't it?' His friend replied smugly, slurring his words and trying, without much success, to parse this idiotically provocative small talk into something that could resemble flirtation. She wasn't having it. They moved down towards the end of the corridor, where they could see a darkened room illuminated periodically by a brilliant pulsating light. The living room was large, sparse and cavernous with a four meter high ceiling; the wallpaper, yellow and dusty, was peeling off at the edges – there were about twenty people standing around, and a few were sitting on the floor at the side. There were three large amplifiers, two battered guitar amps and one bass amp, arranged almost around a circle in the middle of the room; behind them, near the high double windows, there were three floor toms and a bass drum turned to face upwards – a smoke machine, and strobe lights were dotted around the room. Nothing seemed to be happening. His legs were tired and he thought of maybe sitting on the floor, but he felt, unnecessarily but nonetheless, a little self-conscious doing so. He kept standing, swaying gently and unsteady on his feet. He opened the little bottle of cheap whiskey and started drinking it straight. It tasted fucking awful. He looked around the room, mainly to try and get a general idea of the age range – eventually coming to the conclusion that it was acceptable, for him, when he spotted the girl who managed the bar around the corner from him who was, at least, the same age or older than him. She was in his year. Five years since he graduated. Maybe he should go back to study something else? No way. No need. Still no reply. Somebody was smoking weed. Never really got that much into weed. Made him even more paranoid than normal. Maybe he'd be happier if smoked weed regularly? Probably not. *Vous avez bien raison de croire que vous allez mourir, bien sûr.* It really did taste fucking awful. Someone was setting up the synthesiser on some beer-crates in the middle of all of the amps, she pressed a few keys and it was so loud that he could hear his back teeth rattle. He should have called her. He was good on the phone, he thought. Sounded articulate and urbane...probably. Would have been weird just to call her out of the blue a few hours after sleeping together. Maybe he should have waited until tomorrow. Well, it was tomorrow now. Still nothing.

'Maybe you're right, but I suppose I feel threatened. Threatened by a certain class of women who, if I'm completely honest, are solely concerned with power and their own narrow self-interest. I'm surrounded by them, and what have I got to compete with them? Ma Da's an electrician, and even their grandparents went to university. It's not so much that they're women, it's more like a feeling, I dunno, it's impossible to shake it off. Like how a boy from the slums will always instinctively want to throw mud on people whose clothes are cleaner. It's a class thing.' His friend snatched the bottle of whiskey from his hands and took a lengthy gulp.

'Not very convincing, sorry.'

'Well, that's how it is.'

'You still smoke weed right?'

'Unedifying bullshit. Most drugs are at this point.'

'What point?'

'At the point of dealing with consequences.'

'Well?'

'What?'

'It's no a class thing. I don't believe you.'

'How about this…Have you ever thought about how precarious the institution of manhood is? There's nothing natural about manhood, a man isn't just born; men are made into Men – and made with great difficulty. They're conditioned, bolstered, and forced to stand in an upright position through an intricate system of beliefs, suppositions, traditions, and other falsehoods – the entire edifice is likely to collapse at any point. And no one, who eventually becomes a man, is ever entirely comfortable in his position – at every step of his conditioning he feels reluctant and ungrateful for this supposedly privileged role which is being forced on him. He'll never be fully convinced of the need for his role, because he is fundamentally a stubborn, obstinate and lazy creature who wants nothing more than to pursue his own desires and impulses – and the long years of schooling in the ways of manhood are difficult, violent, and utterly brutal. The education is vulgar and cruel in every way imaginable, and in succeeds in making some men equally vulgar and cruel – but most succumb to it with only basic signs of damage and distress, only a minor psychopathology which never becomes psychopathy. A man is a prostrate worm, which the world has expended all its various energies to transform into something more robust. Something which stands upright and marches without complaining. I would be in favour of letting the whole thing collapse, if I didn't believe that it's completely necessary somehow.'

'Right...so you feel threatened?'

'Well I suppose I do. But not for myself.'

'She still hasn't replied.'

'You're still going on about this? Forget about it, she's no gonna reply. It's hard, the feeling, the rejection – but it only lasts as long as you've known her, which in this case is basically only a fraction of a second.'

'But there was a connection....it was a palpable connection.'

'How do you know? You think there's a connection, but she obviously doesn't. Only one of you is right...and it's becoming increasingly unlikely that it's you. Forget about it.'

'How can I forget about it? It's impossible. It seems as if every detail of last night will eventually repeat in my thoughts in an endless loop, and I'll never be able to shake them off. The feel of her skin against my fingers, the sickly sweet honey and blueberries, the nasty wee cat she has, the smile, the lips. Do you think that other men think about these things? You don't seem to care. There must be something wrong with me to be affected like this. I just don't have the temperament to be indifferent to these things – and it's only ever going to make me fucking miserable.'

'Listen, mate, you don't have to worry about that. There's nothing wrong with you. You don't have to make any excuses for being sensitive, and for admitting to being moved by things which most people would pay no attention to. But you need to develop a hardness to survive, for your own sanity, because all these encounters and relationships, they'll just become more and more temporary. It's inevitable. That we're now able to have direct influence on the very nature of the physical world around us, should tell you all you need to know about how important it is to adapt to the pace of acceleration. So, no, there's nothing wrong wi ye. But you will find that people have nae use for your earnest sensitivity, and even less for your sentimentality, however genuinely it may be felt.'

'I'm no sure I'll ever be able tae adapt. I'm hungry for something. I'm always hungry for something. For genuine nourishment. I feel as if I'm slowly starving.' He could tell that his friend had already drifted from the conversation and had begun scanning the room intently and with purpose.

'Yeah, we should have eaten something more. I'm really fucking drunk.' His friend replied.

His mother had once told him that when she was a little girl they were sometimes so short of money that her parents made her go to the butcher to ask for bones for their dog – which they would then boil into broth for their own dinner. It occurred to him that it was certainly a mistake that he should have been formed to think in this way. And formed he was, like many of his friends, in this country – men of a brutalised class, hated and spat upon through all of its history, praised for their courage when thrown to wars, or when it was most convenient; tyrannised from the pulpit and the podium alike. Perhaps a half century ago, his kind would not have had their sensitivities piqued by education – an education given grudgingly by a sententious but predictably fleeting *noblesse oblige*. He had revelled in the hope, once, that somehow he would make them live to regret it. Yet the more educated he became, the more indifferent he became – too little is somehow preferable to too much. Far too much. And what had it got him? Little in the way of approbation, and nothing in the way of material wealth. And less. No longer a sense of belonging, of clinging onto shared injustice. Nothing from home but suspicion and thinly disguised resentment. A life lived in pitiful isolation, sensitive to a world – but powerless to have a hand in it. And what did he know of her life? It was true, he could only speculate – based on the lives of those women whom had held close to his own at one point or another – perhaps she was comparable. She was, after all, of a certain type. Yet there remained something indistinct, an opacity, an inability to distinguish the exact contours and undulations of her thought, her evident suffering, and private madness. If only it were possible to know, definitively, then perhaps their encounter would cease to be so enchanted. For, even in his inebriated state, dejected and without much hope – the promise of that world still seemed so utterly sublime. Nothing comparable.

Three feminine figures in black veils were now ensconced inside the amp circle gripping instruments, with one taller bare-chested man sitting behind the drums at the back. A cacophony of piercing high-pitched screams, heavily distorted and warped, flooded the room as a pounding bass riff bounced against the walls, and between his ears. The drums were hit with violence, in an unforgiving and continuous roll, as the guitar picked out a random atonal staccato. The volume, which was at first overwhelming, seemed of little consequence after a minute or so. Nonetheless, he felt ill at ease.

He escaped out to the corridor, and headed to the kitchen opposite the living room. The light was cold and overly bright, showing too much detail, too much of too many faces and tired features, darks circles, smeared lips, red veiny eyes, wide awake by virtue of alcohol and other chemicals. The blonde girl with the septum piercing was standing by the sink, downing and then re-filling small plastic cups of water. She nodded as he stumbled in her direction, and offered him her cup.

'Drink this', she said, abruptly. 'I used to do some work with your girlfriend. I think we met once or twice. How is she?'

'She's fine.'

'She not coming tonight?'

'No, no, don't think so. She's away.'

'Where is she?'

'In London.'

'What's she doing there?'

'No idea. Working. She isn't my girlfriend anymore.' He replied a little pathetically, looking at the floor.

'Sorry…She was nice.'

'Yeah.'

'Where's your racist friend?'

'Watching the band. He's not racist.'

'Why you saying that? Because you're his friend? Doesn't work like that.'

He attempted to laugh, and assumed she would too – but her face remained stern and without reprieve.

'Drink some more water', she said 'you'll be sick if you don't.'

He took the cup from her again and tried to pour it quickly down his throat, but managed to spill half of it down his mouth and onto his t-shirt.

'Listen', he started slurring, 'Can I ask you something?'

'Yeah.'
'Are you suspicious of men who are sentimental?'
'In what way?'
'Sentimental...you know...feelings and sensations.'
'Most men are sentimental.'
'Genuinely sentimental.' He repeated with pleading emphasis.
'Honestly, I would find it pretty difficult to believe that they're genuine. I'm not really sentimental.'
'Why?'
'I have no interest in the past. The future interests me more. There are less obligations to things which don't mean anything to my life. Nostalgia and sentimentality are constricting and repressive constructs – I don't gain anything from indulging them.'

...

He lay on the bed and looked up at the ceiling. It moved in an elliptical motion, counter-clockwise so that the various water marks and stains on its surface changed position briefly before jerking back to their starting points. He slowly sat up on the bed, and looked around the disordered room; piles of clothes on various chairs, books, records piled up against the walls and out of their sleeves on the floor and on the desk – several ash trays filled to the brim. She stood in front of him at the side of the bed – naked from the waist down, and wearing a black bra. He placed a hand on her thigh, and moved it up and down her leg. When his vision focused, he could see a couple of dark bruises on her legs – the skin was cold, covered in goosebumps and felt rough to the touch. She still sported that vacant expression on her face; neutral, slightly dismissive. She approached the bed and starting removing his trousers, pulling them down to his knees and taking his flaccid cock in her mouth, she began sucking and occasionally biting it. He ran his fingers through her hair, which felt almost synthetic and brittle. She continued for 10 minutes, breathing through her nose, and emitting a low moan now and again – he was finding it difficult to concentrate, feeling uncomfortable, he had strong urge to tell her to stop, as it was becoming clear that he wasn't getting hard. His head was spinning and, on the verge of vomiting, he decided to take matters into his own hands. He gently patted her on the head and took his cock out of her mouth – she removed her bra and lay down on the bed. He stood over her and starting wanking his cock, his head spinning around frantically as the pressure mounted at his temple, and the shame began to magnify. He started fingering her with his right hand, while he held his cock in the other. He closed his eyes and tried to search for some material, something recent – but nothing came to him. He opened his eyes and found that hers were closed – she moaned a little, and bit her bottom lip. He put two fingers inside of her as she got wetter and closed his eyes again and tried to summon some image, something to help him along – but it was impossible. He opened his eyes and looked over her naked body as he increased the firmness of his grip and simultaneously increased the range of the motion of his fingers, a procedure at which – even in such state – he was surprisingly adept. He became momentarily pleased at this newfound knowledge of his own skill, but just as soon returned to a state of panicked distress. He really hadn't wanted to fuck her, but he was going to have to try. Her eyes were open, and she seemed to gesture with a slight move of the head. The nausea returned and he managed to suppress a gag. He took his barely half-erect cock in his hand.

'I need a condom.' He said suddenly, sensing potential to excuse himself.

'I'm on the pill.'

'Erm…ok.' he said, slightly defeated. 'Can't we try in the morning?'

All at once that blank stare fled from her face, and was replaced by one of marked suspicion, hurt and annoyance.

'Is there something wrong?'

'No, nothing…nothing.' He pleaded defensively, as he approached her and grasped her by the waist, pulling her towards him and entering into her. He shut his eyes tight and began thrusting, attempting to summon an image that would alleviate his tangible discomfort; a variety of them came rapidly to his mind, but disappeared just as abruptly. There were too many of them, too many women – mostly women he had never even met, but had consumed nonetheless, and discarded just as readily – the image of those he had known could not help but be mixed up in that maelstrom of flesh, becoming just as indistinct and temporary as their luminous ghostly counterparts; a chaotic mass of pornographic desire which had lost its power to excite and arouse. He lost his erection and withdrew.

'I can't, I'm sorry.'

'What's wrong?' She asked, half flustered, but seeming more surprised and a little upset.

'I'm drunk. I'm too drunk.' He said, bowing his head as he began dressing awkwardly. He turned around to look over that disordered room when he reached the door, and she sat up on the bed, smoking – a blank expression once more on her face. He left with that feeling of distress, of a febrile unease still running amok amongst his thoughts, and added to it a feeling of seediness, of being sullied and polluted.

...

A collection of dark voices could be heard at the peripheries of the borderlandstown – like that film, it's not what it's called but. Going into work like pissing in the jars like what's his name, his Da, the wan that used tae work at the Jam Factory. Mad Alkie, heard him come in tryin tae talk but pure slurring aw the words. Ulrich, Ulrich something – the man with nae *Eigenschaften*. What happened. Got huckled at the weekend, got the jail. You're going to be late! You've missed that train, your feet are not working – not exactly an impact player, but put away a few sometimes. Nothing happened though, she was safe. That girl. There was no one else in the courtyard, and police were looking for her. She had this white room, the walls all painted a certain type of white – a transparent white. I was very worried about her but she seemed so proud. But she did something. We all knew it. She had this room, the white room, it was filled with 25 or 26 plastic bags, see-through bags – filled with blood. Blood. Blood. And piss and shit. When one attempts to appeal on the basis of fact, positive fact, in order to obtain the information to aid us in our enquiries we are then confronted with memory. We should nonetheless expect this, as memory is the intersection of mind and matter, the psycho-physiological relation of the pathological state. There exists no oneness of basic reality – the evidence is abundant, in favour of fragmentation. Many images will come into existence, they will come and go in varying frequencies – but it is vital to simply take one image, the one which is your own body. My body. As you cut it open, what will happen? A cut with the scalpel, cutting through bundles of sinewy fibres – inexplicably bloodless. An insignificant detail. The cut goes through the nerves of the spleen. Is the spleen an actual organ, or is it rather merely a device of shop-worn romantic poetry? No idea. A prostrate worm into something else entirely: "Hi, I guess you're not replying – and I can't figure out why. I can't stop thinking about you, and its absurd for me to feel this – since I know nothing about you, but what I wouldn't give to be close to that knowledge, that knowledge of you, to know your everything." No. Fucking. Way. He awoke with a start, and grabbed at his phone.

…

'The only problem that I can see is how you chose to frame it.' His friend replied.

It's four in the afternoon and his friend, Robert, is lying on the sofa in a ragged grey t-shirt and a pair of Kappa trackie bottoms (poppers) that he's surely had since his early teens, when he must have worn them more baggy. At present they fit snuggly around his crotch; and when he stood up to his full 6ft 4 inches, barely reached down to the bottom of his calves. He's squinting at the laptop which they've insecurely placed at an angle on the coffee table between the two sofas (he's lying on the other, of course), which themselves now sit edge to edge to form an 'L' shape. The screen goes black and the words *Wie soll man leben, wenn man nicht sterben* appeared on the screen. The connection stalls and begins to buffer. Robert groans and rubs his eyes. An advert pops up with a naked dark haired woman in suspenders with drooping breasts that bears a striking resemblance to his primary six school teacher: 'Milfs in your area want to fuck'. He remembered sitting on the floor, drinking milk as they were read a story…and seeing the flash of white panties visible through a tear in the sheer black of her tights. He shudders. The connection rights itself and the subtitles, which are lagging, appear underneath: *How is one to live if one doesn't want to die?* They had made the decision to watch *Berlin Alexanderplatz* in its entirety – a decision which now, only on the second episode and suffering from perhaps the most debilitating hangover of his entire life, seemed to be absurdly wrong-headed. Neither of them, at that point, however, had the inclination or the ability to renege on the decision. There was no food in the house, or at least any which they could be bothered cooking – a pizza had been ordered. Outside, the rain was beating down onto the windows in such a way that it felt as if it were no different from standing outside without an umbrella and being wetted….that is to say, being moistened. No pleasant way to express this. The sound seemed to seep moisture into his every thought, of which there were many, mostly unpleasant, and at that point he was struggling to keep track of them all. Robert had been, hard as it was to imagine, in a much worse state than he had been last night – such a state, in fact, that it now seemed to create something of an intense awkwardness between them which they had never experienced before. He had never seen him in such a state. They had lived together before for three years in their early twenties– when they pissed each other off through disagreements about cleaning habits and various other lapses which seem trifling in retrospect. Thankfully the presence of a third person, a finicky and compulsive introvert – exacting in his vegan diet and spiritual certainty, a compulsively laid-back stoner who was nonetheless forthright in his passive-aggressivity – ensured that their friendship withstood those earlier more turbulent years. No such buffer existed now, he thought with an undue sense of foreboding. In the years that followed, he had always lived with women – and he had never had to deal with the psychic needs of his friends on anything but a superficial level. When they were younger, they often confided in each other readily – but as they had grown old, despite all the heartbreak and despair which had taken place since then – he really knew nothing about him any longer, save for the cutting remarks, banter and ribbing that usually drove their conversations forward.

'I've never been a Rab, or a Bobbie or even a Boab. I think Boab's more east coast though. I used to get called Robbie when I was a bit younger, but then it stopped when I came to Art School. How'd you think it's determined?'

'I dunno, depends what scheme you grew up in.'

'I think it's more arbitrary than that.'

'Maybe you're right.'

On the screen Franz Biberkopf is goaded by his old communist comrades who are singing the *Internationale*, and he stands up to bellow out *The Watch on the Rhine*. Fragments of what he found when he stumbled in from the party come back to him, here and there, between waking up two hours ago and lying on this sofa – and he now seemed to have something approaching the full picture. The front door was ajar after he had struggled up the stairs in the close, the ladder was in the hallway of the flat – above it the smoke alarm was uncovered, with its wires dangling down. The door to the bathroom was locked. He pounded on the door with his fist, since he was bursting for a piss. He could hear some high pitched moans and coughing coming from inside. He banged on the door. A slurred response. 'I really need to piss mate!' He shouted. Some groaning, and the door handle turns meekly, before turning back.

'What's wrong with the way I framed it…apart from the obvious?' He asked

'You know already…' Robert replies.

'Mate, can you just tell me – not in the right state to be fucking arguing wi you.'

'Ok, put it this way…it's no that you sent a stupid drunken text – which in the brief but dishonourable history of drunken texts is comparatively mild – it's more that you didn't even bother framing it in an original way.'

'How should have I put it then?'

'Observe the chaotic rules of the drunken text – throw caution to the wind, come out all guns blazing – tell you fucking love her and you've never met anybody or anything like her in the world, she's incredible, her tits are unbelievable – you wanna thrust yer knob in-between them – or, you know, throw out some of that saccharine poetic wank that you come up with fae time to time. You couldn't even, as pished as you were, go all out drunken text idiotic. That's the problem.'

'Why?'

'You gave her something plausible, and that makes you weaker. There's nothing more pathetic than earnestness.' Robert sat up, and picked up the empty blue glass flower vase that he'd filled to the brim with water and drank at it greedily.

'You got a fag?' He threw an almost empty pack of tobacco onto Robert's lap.

'Really, it makes no difference – because it was fucked anyway. She wisnae gonnae reply. I could have sent anything. I'll never see her again.'

'Aye I'm sure. Because this city is just full of women you sleep with that you'll never see again… You'll bump into her, ye dick. Really, you gottae stop this pathetic behaviour.'

He had eventually gone to the kitchen last night to piss in the sink, making sure to remove all the dirty dishes beforehand. When he'd finished he heard the door to the toilet click open as he walked past, and an extended throaty and painful groan spilled out of the door, against the background of the tinny sound of a woman's high-pitched pig like squeals. He approached cautiously and pushed the door – which was ajar – open. A thick cloud of cigarette smoke filled the room, and the hot water tap was turned all the way up— filling the air with a warm sticky steam. The sink was almost bursting to the brim with roll-up cigarette butts stubbed onto the sides, which were completely yellow. Robert sat with the trousers around his ankles, and his cock gripped firmly in his right hand, awake but barely conscious, with floods of tears falling down his face. The room had an ethanol reek, and there were two big bottles of vodka, one of which was empty, and the other grasped weakly in his left hand. Balanced on the edge of the bathtub was his laptop, on which there was a porn clip playing on full blast. On screen an extremely overweight woman, with several layers of skin fat, seemingly almost immobile on a bed, was being fucked by three men, with two (one underneath and the other on top) fucking her in the arse from behind, stopping occasionally to place her prolapsed colon back inside. The men wore black ski masks. The woman's head was covered in a paper bag with holes torn on the front for the eyes and mouth. When the camera cut to show this, her tongue slid out lizard like through the hole before receding back. He felt physically sick, and could not this time hold back from vomiting in the bathtub. Afterwards he tried as best he could to help Robert get to bed, and unsuccessfully attempted to tidy up the bathroom. Next thing he knew he was awake in his bed, fully clothed. Presently, he felt ashamed to even remember his friend like this – though it had only occurred a few hours before. It didn't seem right for him to have this repugnant memory – to allow it equal placement amongst those which he remembered with warmth and pride. At that point he somehow wanted to embrace him, but this thought itself was fleeting. Franz Biberkopf delivers an extended monologue, lamenting that nobody can understand what it was like for him in prison.

So, what was the lesson here? What had he learned? He had no answer to this question at present. There was, in fact, no discernible answer to this question. It was entirely possible that she already had a boyfriend. It was true that there didn't seem to be any evidence of his presence anywhere in her flat…but maybe they didn't live together. Perhaps he lived in a completely different city, and they only saw each other occasionally. He was, obviously, much better looking and taller than him – with the dress sense, clothes and mannerisms indicative of firm bourgeois breeding, but at pains to hide these origins. He was probably a graffiti artist, or something of a suitably proletarian affectation…but bullshit. English, obviously. The ability to grow more facial hair than he could, on a mere whim, but clean shaven most of the time. His hands were far more elegant and soft than his. She became a completely different person around him; she became clumsier and not as confident. He made her feel inadequate, the prick. He obviously did it on purpose. But his mere presence could make her laugh. He always looked right into her eyes when he was fucking her and always made sure that she came, every time, without fail. Well, what had it come to in any case? She didn't love him anymore…but maybe it would take a while to get over this boyfriend. Either way, there wasn't much of a chance for him.

    Robert got up and tapped on the laptop. The screen goes black again: *Ein Hammer auf den Kopf kann die Seele verletzen*. The connection buffers again. It starts back up with a jerk; *A hammer blow to the head can injure the soul*, the subtitle reads. Swarming microbial superstitions, these are what governed the interactions and games – untested hypotheses, speculation, counter-intuitive actions and chance. Only the last factor really had any tangible impact. The reasons why such things work out, disintegrate or progress were often simple enough, but the truth is much less preferable than the comfort of delusion. He reached forward, closed the laptop and sat up on the sofa. Robert didn't move at all.

'I cannae be fucked wi this.'

'How else will we pass the time?'

'Dunno…What happened with you last night?' He asked, regretting it slightly, '…at the party'.

'I tanked a bottle of vodka I found in the kitchen then I blacked out, don't remember getting home. Nothing of note. What about you?'

'I got off with that girl who was on the door.'

'Cherie?'

'Cheree? Like the song?'

'No, like the name. It's a name.'

'You know her?'

'I know folk that know her.'

'Then why were you being such a dick to her?'

'It's often more fun than not being a dick. Anyway, yeah – so what happened?'

'I'm not sure exactly.'

'You like her?'

'She's seems like a nice person.'

'Did anything happen?'

'Not exactly.'

'Occupational hazard, ma man. What did you talk about?'

'I think she was of the opinion that sentimentality is now an exclusively masculine phenomenon.'

'A bold assertion.'

'I wasn't entirely convinced.'

'Well, if the sample cross-section contains mawkish cunts like you – then perhaps she has a point. Anyway, that can't be all that was discussed?'

'I'm no sure, my mind was elsewhere…Something about this sentimentality being a symptom of a lament for lost privilege.'

'Here…I'm pretty sure she went to Hutchie Grammar.'

The conversation had begun to have an effect on Robert, as he became more animated and appeared to be devoting more of his attention. Now he had also sat up and was busy rolling another cigarette between his fingers; little by little he was beginning to regain his usual demeanour, an imperious insouciance that always succeeded in convincing anyone who spoke with him that he was troubled by very little in his day to day – and that if he could somehow impart this practised indifference to you, it would reveal the triviality of your own problems. There was a feeling that even if he suffered any specific conflicts or upheavals, he would never consciously nor deliberately reveal them to anyone. It was a quality which he envied in his friend. Discussions such as these were almost invariably one-sided; Robert would listen attentively and would appear to take a genuine interest in these problems – but ultimately the sense was that his interest was only temporary and of the moment. Even in outward appearance, he had a quality of sturdiness and solidity, despite his extended length and slenderness. Robert was almost always at least a head taller than most other people in the room, and a least three inches taller than himself. When he was sober his movements were precise and graceful and never unnecessary – he had no tics, no mannerisms to speak of; no nervous leg-shaking, no tapping of the feet or drumming of the fingers, his gait was measured and never rushed. When he shook someone's hand, he had a habit of crushing the phalanxes together, usually causing the other person to flinch. When they had first met he had thought this to be a transparent power play – but now he was entirely convinced that his friend was completely unware of the pain he was inflicting.

'I once saw her exhibiting, she used tae paint – I don't think she does anymore. A friend told me that something happened tae her a coupla years back, an episode. They were mostly figurative, the paintings. If I remember right though, they were blurred portraits of naked human bodies, but they were misshapen and contorted in various ways. The texture of her brush was quite delicate and she had this astute sense of form, and a real sensitivity for colour.'

'You trying to make me feel bad?'

'No intentionally, no. Just saying…her painting was extremely self-reflexive. Even if she isn't now – she was at one point in her life, intensely sentimental.'

'Well, I do feel bad.'

'It's no such a big deal, there are worse ways to spend your time than balls deep in the daughters of the bourgeoisie. Played two, scored two. A pretty solid record.'

'Played two, scored one.'

'Played two, scored one – another was disallowed.'

'Played two, scored one, and then got sent off.'

'Did she send you off?'

'I think I just left.'

'Played two, scored one, missed a sitter, then got injured and taken off. Still, not a bad record. An impact player.'

'I was wasted, and I really couldn't get my head in the game.'

'Then why did you bother?'

'I don't even know how it happened and if I'm completely honest, I feel awful about it.'

'Why?'

'It's a strange feeling to describe, and I'm not sure if I'm even capable.'

'You're hardly the first person to fail in this way. Nothing tae feel bad about.'

'The failure isn't what I feel awful about…ah canny really account for this feeling of…distress.'

'Is it distress or is it disgust?'

'…'

'It's probably just the hangover. And it's Sunday. I don't think I can ever remember feeling optimistic on a Sunday.'

'Lately, I have found it…disgusting, sometimes.'

'Ok…Played two, scored one – missed a penalty, and announced your retirement before the game was finished.'

Outside the rain had stopped, and he could see the streetlights beginning to switch on. The pizza arrived late; once they opened it up…the fat had started to coagulate into a white powdery paste onto the pieces of brown kebab meat on its surface. They put a few slices into the microwave until the cheese and oil sizzled and crusted at the edges. They sat down to eat in the kitchen and were mostly silent. He could only manage to eat half a slice before the nausea got the better of him. Robert was, of course, not always like this. A few years before there was a woman, Laura, a researcher in evolutionary biology, who he met before he started doing his PhD. The two of them had been inseparable. She was very small compared to him, almost half of his sizeable length, but very assertive and abrasive – difficult to sustain friendly conversation with, prone to offence and incapable of taking a joke at her own expense, though quick to highlight other people's shortcomings and failings. She was beautiful in a bland way, all blonde hair and delicate features, but with a certain sourness that detracted from these obvious allures. She revelled in drama, caused it on a whim, but was often incredulous when it seemed to follow her around. She looked always on the point of a tantrum, even when happy and contented – a perennial and never ending huff. Never having been told anything otherwise, she was convinced of her superiority and aptitude for the managerial. It was obvious that she had a very stubborn intelligence, clearly substantial, yet it was mired by her over-reliance on conventional wisdom and the mores of her solidly middle class family; ambitious and venal in equal measures. She wasn't without her specific charms, loquacious and expansive in company – but in private, among those she considered close, this resulted in a judgemental deportment. She gave the impression of always striving against injustice and oppression, and was always among the first to perform her outrage. But it soon became apparent that her sole concern in doing so was to draw attention to her moral superiority, which in reality, was tenuous at best. She was disingenuous as a reflex, and everything she did and said was in the service of attaining the goal she had in mind for herself.

 Nevertheless, Robert loved her a great deal. It was, at first, quite difficult to understand how such a pairing came about, or for that matter how it lasted for the years that they were together. They constantly spent time with each other, and it was volatile from the outset – they would argue constantly, and this seemed to be the functional basis of their relationship: it appeared to sustain them. Each seemed to relish this constant friction. After some time, however, and particularly towards the end, Robert seemed to relent and became mostly silent in her company. It was impossible to see him without her, whenever he was invited anywhere, she would always be there with him. Their conversations were punctuated by rare snide remarks directed at one another, but they scarcely seemed to acknowledge each other's presence – an axiomatic disquiet permeated their dealings. Eventually they had quite a rancorous parting caused by multiple infidelities, and one transmission of chlamydia. Since then, in his subsequent and short lived relationships with women, Robert had been at pains to present an image of himself as unencumbered and unattached – successfully if not convincingly attempting to embody some outdated mode of swagger-sex. But after a while, he had abandoned this too, and seemed to prefer his solitude above all else.

'You remember Alan fae uni?' Robert asked with his mouth full.

'No really.'

'I used to knock about wi him for a while in first year. Wee nerdy guy wi the beard, you'd see him at gigs all the time, always had digits on him – used to play in that math rock band.'

'Oh aye. Really awkward guy?'

'Aye, that's him. He's dead…he was on holiday on this Greek island, right, and he hired a moped. Rode it aff a cliff.'

'On purpose?'

'Probably. Doesn't really matter, does it? It was probably for the best.'

'How?'

'I always thought he must be fucking miserable. He always tried hard, but for what? But in the end, he kept it for himself, his death, and he never let any cunt take it from him. It takes a certain pride in your own existence to kill yourself, I reckon. It's the strongest weapon a man has, his own death. But you can only dae it once, so you have tae make it count.'

After they had eaten, he took two Xanax and went to lie down in his bed. The worst effects of the hangover had already begun to subside, leaving only a dull throbbing pain at his temple – the intensity of his fevered emotions had also begun to lessen, leaving a more manageable but nonetheless glaring feeling of despondency. There was, of course, no lesson to be learned – no knowledge that he will carry forward into the future in the hopes of approaching another similar situation with hard won wisdom, somehow willing the outcome to be different. The willing is all: the be all and end all. How could he judge the authenticity of these sensations which had, in such a short space of time, he could now honestly admit, engulfed him completely? It was obvious that what had occurred was merely another arbitrary and random occurrence, opportune for that moment in time, but essentially random. To ascribe any form of meaning would be to admit, in effect, to being vulnerable to those capricious notions of cosmic pre-determination…and he always had nothing but contempt for such beliefs. But to be hungover, he thought bitterly, is the closest one will ever come to a Damascene conversion. As he stared up at the ceiling he drifted in and out of sleep; some blurry spectres were dancing mockingly on its surface, before the whole room was consumed by an enveloping darkness.

…

The Langfield Film Archive had opened around 5 years ago, built into (and through) a disused building in the middle of an older industrial estate in the Southside. The large red sandstone building was as tall as a four floor tenement and stretched another three blocks across the length of the street. There was very little else around, no shops or other functioning buildings in use – down on the end of the street was a large empty piece of wasteland with abandoned furniture, broken glass, rubbish and syringes. Occasionally there were a group of junkies who congregated on the corner next to this area, to which they had dragged a sofa and a couple of chairs. On several occasions, when he was walking into work in the morning, he would see some of them defecating openly. People had once lived in the nearby tenements, but all of them had now been boarded up – and the couple which had been burnt out were in the process of being slowly torn down. Only the façade of this building, once a poorhouse serving the parish – all pompous second rate baronial battlements and miniature spires – now remained. The building had been entirely gutted and renovated. The roof had had several large holes punctured through it, plugged up by glass skylights which had the effect of making the interior – which was painted entirely white – impeccably luminous and airy. Inside, all of the equipment, computers, and furnishings seemingly remained permanently new – but were at any rate replaced every two years. The building had three floors which were open plan, with a large brushed steel and glass spiral staircase in the middle. It was, he had thought when he first began this job, entirely contrary to what you would assume a film archive would look like; and such a presumption would turn out to be correct in some way. For the Langfield was a film archive which didn't seem to have a definite purpose. There was, including himself, 12 employees within the huge cavernous expanse of this light filled building – all of whom, with the exception of himself and the Director, rather inexplicably had some form of managerial function; managers of outreach, public engagement, communications, collections optimisation, marketing, corporate responsibility, sustainability and 'projects.' Most of them were either around his age, or a bit older, a more or less equitable balance of gender, though certainly more women. Most rode their bikes over the bridge from the West End, or drove in from Pollokshields, Newlands and Bearsden. They all seemed to know each other from somewhere else. The Director, a youthful looking middle-aged man with thick greying hair, had a habit of wearing light beige tweed suits, and immaculately pressed white shirts which always seemed fresh. He wore thin silver steel framed glasses and drove a 1960s bottle green Iso Rivolta. Something in his manner and his pleasantly understated Perthshire accent gave the impression of a military bearing – but the Director had, apparently, worked for years on international development projects in water, sanitation and hygiene around the Congo Basin.

He worked as a collections assistant, the theoretical bottom rung of a loosely constructed and largely incomprehensible hierarchy which he had still not bothered to learn. In effect, this meant he had the job of viewing, cataloguing and digitising the footage which was stored discreetly in cupboards and drawers in the large glass fronted, climate controlled archive room on the bottom floor. In this huge chilly room, which was also sound-proofed, there was one partially concealed corner which was hidden behind three imposingly tall steel cupboards. This was where he had his desk and sat for two days a week, wearing a thick jumper in all seasons and sometimes a long overcoat – converting hours and hours of grainy and mostly uninteresting footage. The purpose of the Archive was putatively related to the history of the area, built rapidly and zealously with a generous injection of government funds and private donations, the 'Terms of Reference' for the project (which he had once managed to access in the shared filing system, before it disappeared) called for a 'permanent space to explore and celebrate the unique character of the people of this area, who were so vital to the industrial culture of the city'. The archive was accessible to the public without appointment; a handful of researchers, artists and academics came in to browse the catalogue every month – spent a couple of hours in the viewing booths – and left. Curiously, aside from these people, his colleagues took little interest in the contents of the archive. In any case, digitised copies of the most noteworthy footage from the Langfield – too fragile to be transported – were also kept in the National Film Archive in the capital. He was mostly left to his own devices and took the opportunity – and the presence of all of this equipment – to surreptitiously work on his own film project.

 He had been working on it for almost four years. To call it a project may give the impression that it was a work which had an end goal in mind, a narrative arc or a coherent structure. What it actually amounted to was a collection of hundreds of shots, of varying lengths (the longest was no more than 5 minutes); some impressions he had gathered, some loosely scripted scenes with bit parts acted by friends; vignettes, flashes of colour, conversations on which he had eavesdropped, or interactions between people he had clandestinely filmed. His previous and only complete work was a documentary. He had gone around the last remaining British Legion clubs in the city, filming interviews with older military veterans while they drank at the club and talked about their various tours of duty. Sometimes he would be invited into their homes for lunch, and they would serve corn-beef sandwiches and show all of the souvenirs they had gathered; knives, machetes, one shrunken head of questionable authenticity, bloodied uniforms, pistols, AK47s, grenades, and an inordinate number of plastic dolls salvaged from the rubble of war-zones. The culmination was a V.E day celebration where all of the veterans – from the different services, some of them in faded Mess Dress – marched in formation to a full brass band inside the small flat topped concrete pub in a scheme somewhere in Shettleston, singing *Lili Marlene*, *White Cliffs of Dover* and *We'll Meet Again* and drinking until the early hours. The resulting footage was, entirely by accident, languidly transcendent. Afterwards himself and Robert (who he'd asked to do the sound) got jumped by a few of the younger guys, not veterans but regulars at the pub nonetheless, who had been hanging around and didn't like the way they looked and had assumed (correctly, as it happens) that they were catholic. 'You know my parents had a mixed marriage?' Robert had remarked nonchalantly, through his fat and bloody bottom lip afterwards when they were waiting to be seen in the A&E. 'My Granda on my Maw's side was a mason, worked as a glazer…replaced all the windows in the People's Palace once… died from cirrhosis…insisted he could tell a catholic by the kind of haircut he had.' The end product was long-listed for a regional award, received a couple of small but well-received screenings… then nothing. He had a broken nose and bruised ribs for quite a while afterwards. Six months later, though not consciously, he started to cut his hair a little differently.

Today he felt awful and was unable to concentrate. He had spent the last three hours trying to edit a clip he had filmed a couple of months ago. He managed to capture a fight develop between a group of men outside of a pub – something which started as a simple enough misunderstanding but escalated quickly into a physical altercation. He was at the time, visiting a friend who lived on the third floor – the flat looked down onto the side entrance of the pub – a pub which was generally salubrious, and not known to be a venue for violence. The window was open, but as the entrance to the pub must have been around 50 yards away, it was impossible to follow the exact specifics of the dispute in which four men were involved, until it concluded in a clamour of screamed insults, the sound of smashing glass, followed shortly after by the approach of the inevitable police siren, which scattered all participants to the winds. He was on the point of deleting it altogether. The most persistent of his creative problems, of which there were many, was an inability to maintain consistency. This was exasperated by a marked obsession with the theoretical, which hindered a highly astute and intuitive aesthetic feeling – a sensibility which he nonetheless felt was too easily interpreted. He had, above all, a dread of producing work which was easy; easily consumed, easily subsumed and easily assimilated. As a result, although he always aimed for some form of mythical universality, and seemed furthermore to have an innate capacity for it, the end result would always be interspersed with many layers of involuntary irony, dissonance and indeterminacy. The very heart of this problem, he felt, was plausibility – which in itself was absurd. The question of what is plausible shouldn't have any influence on the matter – as the form which he had finally settled on, reflecting and capturing reality, does not require a verdict on credibility. But he had never felt credible, and this was the problem; in all of the different scenes that had made up the narrative of his own paltry life, among all the countless visceral spectacles of distress, even when their effect on him was direct, a feeling of unreality and implausibility prevailed. Despair at this philosophical proposition had plagued him not only in his film making efforts, but in all of the other things which he had attempted in the past; in music, writing, and a brief foray into painting. It was perhaps the only thing which, many years ago, had made him contemplate suicide, something which he lacked both the courage and determination to attempt. Besides, the urge never much felt real either – never completely plausible or credible.

On the few occasions that he could get beyond what he genuinely knew to be nothing more than a debilitating solipsism, he could perceive the coordinates of a more comprehensive societal problem. There were, as far was he could see, two antagonistic philosophies of life – one which follows a mystic form of cognition which, at its most tangible, is expressed in one type of faith…this mode of existence has apparently become archaic, despite its numerous manifestations outside of what are customarily referred to as beliefs – the religious sentiment pervades a great deal, still, even in the avowedly irreligious. Opposed to this is a negation, a perfectly self-conscious form of revolt against the former…delimited, and fixated with an almost diabolical apotheosis of the profane, the merging of organic and machinic desire as it is optimistically articulated by those maladroit victims of modern *ressentiment*. Both are forms of faith, and neither are plausible…we no longer possess the requisite intransigence, the quietist conviction that comes with fanaticism

– a passion born of ignorance, but which proved itself time and again to be more than capable of transcending it.

So, he couldn't concentrate. And also because…because, early this morning when he was walking into work, he had finally received a reply. 'Phone was broken…let's talk later', was all that it said. Of course the mere fact of receiving a reply had buoyed his spirits, and made him giddy with excitement – albeit only temporarily. Nevertheless, after a couple of hours he began to feel apprehensive again. He couldn't, after all, be certain if the reply was intended to be dismissive. Given how circumspect and brief it was, this was entirely possible. In addition, as is common on a Monday, after a weekend's worth of hard drinking, his despondency had somehow transmuted into an intense and acute embarrassment. If he was able to consider these feelings from a position of disinterestedness, from the outside, he would rapidly come to conclusion that such feelings were completely unwarranted – but at that moment, he was incapable of being so objective.

He thought it was probably best not to contact her again. His pride had been wounded. Had he known, when he was younger, that he would come to expend this much intellectual energy in analysing the minutiae of random romantic encounters – he may have acted differently; been less insensitive with the feelings of others, made more of an effort to work on building enduring connections… Perhaps it was time to retire? Celibacy in its contemporary form was a vastly different prospect from what it previously was. It was entirely possible to live a life without intimacy, free from any meaningfully debilitating sexual frustration. He had, after all, produced enough memories to reflect upon and assuage his potent sense of nostalgia and weakness for the sentimental. This line of reasoning was obviously disingenuous, but nevertheless he clung onto the illusion for the rest of the afternoon. And even when he eventually got home after work, and right up until the moment when she picked up the phone with an audible mixture of surprise and excitement, he could still glimpse that remote abode of work and pure delight steadily receding into the distance.

III

WOMAN AS WATERFALL

He got on a bus but immediately regretted it. It was moving too slowly for one thing, and it was nearly empty, or not nearly empty enough – nothing to focus his attention on nor any opportunity to retreat completely. He put in his earphones and tried to focus on the music. The sound of screeching trebly feedback and the distant drums of *The Living End* made it unquestionably worse; his vision was starting to blur and his mouth was so dry that he felt his tongue catching on the back of the throat – he took a massive swig of the big water bottle he bought at the corner shop before getting on the bus. How many stops was he going? This was ridiculous… what would happened if he stayed on the bus? Something felt like it was going to happen. But nothing was happening. He tried to find another Mary Chain song and pressed the shuffle button, something more soothing…well if he got off the bus now, and then just walked to some alleyway or street corner, then he could faint, or collapse, or whatever it was he felt like he was in danger of doing, in peace, without any embarrassment, but it'd be pretty embarrassing if he just got off though – he asked the driver to shout the stop, so if he just got off there'd be questions…inevitably. He took a long gulp of the water bottle, a big fat stubby litre bottle which was almost empty now….could he drown from drinking too much water? 'Better to paint my head on the walls before the picture goes'…he had to find something else…piano, classical….a nocturne. The bus had only gone three stops...another 7 to go. He started sweating, or at least it felt like he was sweating. A couple of guys got on, they looked familiar and stared at him suspiciously as they took their seats. They probably think he's on something... they'll tell the driver, who's going to stop and maybe throw him off the bus. Didn't he need to get off the bus anyway? But then he'd be late. He started discreetly but violently pinching his forearms, gripping the skin between his nails (he needed to cut his nails) on his thumb, index and middle fingers. This is pretty fucking stupid, it won't matter if you're late...why did you forget the pills though? Didn't need them. Just try to remember the last time you were on a bus. Never liked buses. Sitting in the middle of the school bus while they all got rowdy sitting in the back...but he never sat at the front, always somewhere around the middle, still within both spheres of influence. Looking right down to the end of the aisle and seeing Burch sitting in the middle, both beefy muscular arms resting on the two empty seats on either side of him. Thomas Burch, John Burch, David...it didn't matter, apparitions don't have first names; stubble, shadows under pale serpent eyes, veins pulsating on either temple, closely cropped hair, broad and barrel chested – fully grown malevolence, a man inexplicably set loose among children – though only 16 years old. He spoke with a raspy monotone....or through the little mouthy wee cunt he used as his interlocutor. Somebody messed with this wee guy once when Burch was off school. The next day when he was back, he grabbed the hapless kid by the scruff of the neck and rag-dolled him around, cracking the plastic walls of the bus stop. Years later when he went back home in the summer before he graduated university, he was walking home from the pub one night...then, as now, and just as suddenly, an atmosphere of impending terror had gripped him, a terror unlike any other before, and one he had never previously imagined – he ran as fast as he could as a primeval howling broke the silence of that uneasy night. Later, he read that Burch had got into a fight outside the nightclub down the road…he stamped on a guy's head repeatedly until the skull had cracked like wet rotten wood. He was sent to prison for 18 years. Still another three stops left. The bus stopped at a traffic light, and began shaking and pulsating. He leaned his head onto the window in the hopes that the vibrations could somehow also shake the terror out of his brain...or re-jig its chemistry through brute force. It's still stopped, the bus. Maybe it's stalled, and the engine had given way – the doors are locked, impossible to get out, noxious gas would fill the interior and they would all choke to death. Well, death would be a welcome respite at this point. Still not too late, he could jump to his feet and pull the emergency handle – and just run…run to the place to meet her – maybe if he sprinted fast enough he could pop into a bar, down a double whiskey, calm down, and still be on time. What would he say when he met her, should he give her a hug – or a kiss on the cheek, or a pat on the back (bit weird)….the fuck was he going to talk about? When did cunts start going on dates? Seems like you never ever went on one before, and now that's all any cunt does. Like almost every other facet of this insipid cultural hegemony and the lexicon it had come with…Yankee go home! Was this a date though? Nobody had said the word 'date'. Perhaps it wasn't a date. He felt the outline of the jonny in his pocket. Always overly optimistic, despite himself. It was beginning to subside…but the panic only needed the smallest impetus to regain possession of him. Fortunately he was able to hold it at bay. Finally when the bus arrived, he sprang to his feet and descended – and once he was on the street, the debilitating turmoil which had passed just a moment before seemed so utterly trifling that he could barely contain his own laughter.

He entered the gallery space and headed straight towards the refreshment table, grabbing a bottle of warmish beer, and throwing a few loose coins into the donation box before downing it hastily. He was confronted with many familiar looking faces, some of whom he had interacted with – a couple of them he knew only by sight, or through reputation and rumours, both scurrilous and sympathetic. He took a little turn around the space – it wasn't huge, but fit around 40 people comfortably inside. It smelled strongly of freshly dried paint and white spirit. The gallery was located in the East, on a periphery, one or two doors within a narrow strip that perched uncomfortably among its surroundings – another outpost of progress that would, timidly but with a certain degree of inevitability, edge further eastward when conditions were conducive. When she had asked him to come tonight the invitation wasn't exactly enthusiastic. He caught her in the corner of his eye, chatting to a couple; the man (perhaps in his early forties) with a grey woollen flat cap perched on top of his bald head, and a woman, slightly younger than the man, with sandy hair and dark bug-like eyes who wore a pink pashmina around her bony shoulders. She waved when she caught sight of him and walked over gradually in a fluid motion, a wide beaming smile across her face. She hugged him momentarily. 'Have you had your dinner?' She asked, and without waiting for him to answer she turned on her heel, rushed over to the table, and grabbed a fistful of pretzel sticks from a small bowl before walking back over and thrusting them into his hands.

'Oh, let's go and have dinner somewhere afterwards…I'm starving!' He walked over to the table and grabbed another two beers.

'Can you show me the work?'

'Mumh mumh mumh bwah beh.' She replied, screwing up her face and laughing.

'Sorry?'

'You mumble a lot!'

'I asked if you could show me the work?'

'Yeah, I'm sorry...I think it's cute.'

They walked over to a set of four large photographs hanging in a row on the wall nearest to the window. He coughed, and cleared his mouth.

'Who are the models?' He asked. She became contemplative and paused, looking over the prints carefully.

'Well, the one at the beginning and the end – that's the arse of the artist...and I think that the other is the arse of his boyfriend. Do you like them?'

'It's an interesting vignetting effect...its like erm, a sort of tenebroso technique.'

'I mean the arses. Do you like them?'

'They're quite hairy, but yeah – I mean, it's quite revealing and...visceral. Oh, and I see there's a glimpse of ball sack there as well...And what's this painting over there?'

On the adjacent wall hung a large unframed canvas, stuck with pins onto the plain white wall. It depicted a figure of an old man in greys and browns, dressed in waistcoat and shirtsleeves pointing upwards from a low-to-high perspective; only his head, arms and shoulders are visible – his hands, in which he is holding something on which his attention is fixated, blur and fade until they blend into the background, a mixture of murky gold and dusty yellow. The detail, intricate and deliberate (but slightly careless), seemed to suggest that it was painted from memory.

'Do you like it?' She asked.

'Very much.'

'It's very sweet, I suppose. Do you want to smoke or are you still unwell?'

'No....I mean...no I'm not unwell. Let's smoke.'

There was a slight drizzle outside, so they huddled underneath the doorway. She placed two cigarettes in her mouth and lit them, before reaching up and placing one of them between his lips. He took a drag, and when it hit the back of his throat his entire chest convulsed for a few moments with a dry hacking cough. She looked puzzled at first, but then gave him three fairly sharp pats on the back. She wore tight dark blue jeans and a black jumper, her hair was tied up in a singular French plait which didn't move, and seemed to pull the skin around her forehead back - imparting a certain severity to her eyebrows, which had been plucked quite recently and dramatically. He was at a loss for conversation and with each passing instant the need to interject became more and more pressing - but he couldn't, nonetheless, think of anything to say, and had mostly to avoid her questioning and increasingly impatient gaze. At that particular moment, he was gripped by a sensation of nausea – of sea-sickness, an imbalance in his legs – the pavement felt unsteady underneath his usually sturdy boots; recollections of their communication in the past few days came in progressively larger waves of disquietude...despite her smile, and her hospitable laugh – she hadn't really wanted him to be here, he couldn't help but feel. He took another long drag of the cigarette.

'I'm sorry about those texts...I ended up getting pretty drunk over the weekend.'

'Which texts?'

'The ones I sent over the weekend.'

'Hhhmm...my phone was broken, don't think I got all of them.'

'Which...', he paused for a moment and took the last few drags of the fag and stubbed it out. She seemed not to be paying much attention, and was looking through the window into the interior of the gallery – where some assistants were placing chairs in four rows in front of a small white table with a microphone in the middle.

'How was your weekend anyway?' He asked her.

'It was ok, but I think Rosie has a stomach bug or something, she keeps vomiting – I need to take her to the vet. So do you get that drunk every weekend?'

'Sometimes…well a lot recently…most weekends to be fair.'

'That's a bit, I dunno, puerile isn't it?' She asked, wrinkling her nose.

'Well, what do you do with your weekend?' He replied, with slight annoyance.

'I don't get totally blootered, anyway. What's the point? It's a waste of time. You're obviously not lacking in imagination, so why do you feel the need to go out and get wasted? Are you trying to forget about something?'

'No, not especially. I wouldn't read too much into it, you're not likely to find much. It's just boredom. Or maybe it *is* a lack of imagination…I don't know why you're so bothered about it.'

'Because it isn't good for you!' She exclaimed.

Her cheeks had become flushed with a reddish hue, and she seemed visibly angry. He was a little taken aback by her outburst, and couldn't quite figure out whether it was genuine. Still, he felt incapable of letting it slide and had himself become pretty annoyed.

'Aside from the obvious things, which aren't really an issue… because I'm not an alcoholic – I don't drink compulsively or because I'm unable to stop, I'm not addicted. Obviously it's not good for me….but it's not that bad. Also…you were pretty drunk the night we met. Don't really get the moralising here…its weirdly puritanical.'

'Ok fine. Maybe I'm puritanical. Occasionally, its fine – obviously…But you said that you were, that you don't feel…and to be honest you look little unwell, you're quite pale and look exhausted...I just have an issue with this. I think it's stupid.'

She reached into the pocket of her jeans and pulled out a blue and white metal case. Taking the lid off, she took some of the balm and rubbed it onto her lips – and then taking a small amount onto her index finger – she stepped closer to him, and softly dabbed it onto his lips and rubbed it in.

'Your lips are really dry.'

When they headed back inside, people had already started to sit down on the assembled chairs. Some, for whatever reason, had decided to sit on the floor – others had removed chairs from the edges of the rows, and moved them a couple of paces out of alignment, and sat at an angle. At the table, the bald man with the cap (now removed) was looking over some notes. She selected two seats in the middle of one row, which made him momentarily panic and take a large swig of his flat beer. He sat closest to the end, three seats – currently unoccupied – away from an exit route, which was partially blocked by a pillar. His legs were shaking restlessly, and he stared down at them – then down at her legs, which were crossed and perfectly still. He noticed that she was sitting at a slight angle away from him. The bald man cleared his throat and everybody fell silent. He introduced himself with the hint of an accent that seemed a little affected – the curator such and such of the...he stopped shaking his legs. He glanced over at her for a brief second, and she was concentrating on reading the hand-out. The curator started talking, and she looked up towards the front. He slowly edged his left leg over towards her, until his knee was brushing ever so slightly against hers – and kept it there. She moved her leg away briefly, and then back again. She then placed a hand on his leg, squeezed it lightly, and started drumming her fingers on his kneecap in an erratic staccato rhythm, never taking her eyes from the front. He edged his hand cautiously closer, and placed it over hers. 'Conceptual praxis is a zero-sum game within the confines of this particular urban environment, born out of violence, poverty and dissipation – it used these as its rhizomatic lessons and referents. The patterns and functions of this game have been continually transmogrified according to emergent social contexts – and are thus not immutable. What then is the role of the critic, the arborescent arcane figure, now adrift in an evolving environment of proliferating multiplicities, each of which demands central attention? The idealistic and teleological vision of a progressive conceptual praxis has, of late, become suspect – justifiably confronted by varying arrays of classes, spaces and a diversity of bodies.' He let out an involuntary sigh – and she turned to him with a brief look of bemusement which may or may not have been annoyance. 'The current era', the curator continued, 'must be solely concerned with emancipation – all concerns which do not derive from it should be treated with suspicion…emancipation from the various constraints which afflict the individual as they once constrained form. Ours is a promethean era, one of accelerated progress, it is therefore incumbent upon us to be worthy of it – praxis must embrace all of these multiplicities simultaneously, incorporating them within its conceptual frameworks, making them more relational, user-friendly, and interactive. Any objection to this is inherently elitist.' At this, there was a subdued round of applause – only lasting a second or two – before the curator continued. Meanwhile, he could feel his leg becoming restless again, and he felt all at once that something was about to happen. He was finding it difficult to follow the presentation by this bald curator – but at the same time, he didn't want her to think of him as ignorant and unappreciative of the invitation. The curator wasn't a large man, not tall and not particularly broad, but his body seemed to occupy a large area of

103

space nonetheless. He wore thick round frame glasses and a navy suit jacket made of a soft wool blend over a black and white polo shirt. On his fingers were a couple of gold rings; a tattoo, black and green, could be glimpsed on the underside of his forearm, and small letters – CYKA – on the knuckles of the hand holding the paper, from which he was still reading enthusiastically. He looked around at the audience; the woman with the bug-like eyes and pink pashmina (now removed) was sitting off to the side near the front. Perhaps it was the curator's wife, he thought. He drank the last drops of beer left in the bottle, and placed it carefully at his feet. There was a noise at the front door, which was behind him and slightly to the left – somebody was having some trouble opening it. He looked over distractedly and saw a diminutive older man with slightly hollowed looking cheeks and a head of matted grey hair saunter in, cautiously at first, but then with a definite swagger towards the refreshment table. The little old man, dressed in an oversized black wind-breaker, grabbed himself a beer, and walked over to where the talk was happening. For a few moments he appeared to be contemplating where to sit down…but in the end he just seemed to prefer hovering a couple of paces back from the last row. His alcoholic reek filled the room quickly. The curator, who was now on his feet for some reason, didn't seem to notice the newcomer and continued with his presentation:

'Anything which does not subscribe to a certain communicability will in time vanish, since this is the absurd and inequitable logic of the market – the intrinsic flaw in a system which has itself become impossible to communicate with any degree of accuracy without recourse to irony and delusion. But what is required is an immanent critique….to use the functions and anti-logic of absurdity in the pursuit of the sublime.'

'Here, Big Man…'

'What is the alternative? Planetary climactic peril, annihilation – species wide extinction, that is the ultimate horizon of existence, or non-existence in the case of the latter. The sooner we face and embrace this inevitable reality, the sooner we can unleash our promethean potential. This potential requires a radical accelerated praxis, and a radical criticism.'

'Here, Big Yin.' The little old man repeated. The curator, who was in-between points, stopped briefly. There was another round of applause, but it was even more subdued this time around. Members of the audience looked around at each other, and towards the speaker, who appeared a bit agitated.

'Big Man...here, you up front there. Whits aw this yer oan about? Wit kind a poetry readings this? It's no exactly John Cooper Clarke...need tae put a bit more emphasis oan yer errr diction... yer bloody dick-shin.' The little old man exclaimed, slurring his words a little, but sporting a rather good natured and warm smile.

'An accelerated praxis....is...'

'What's he oan about?' The little old man gesticulated towards the audience. One or two of them looked round anxiously, unsure of how to respond.

'It's err...it's not a poetry reading. Questions at the end please.' The curator piped in awkwardly – removing his glasses and cleaning them on the sleeve of his jacket.

'Aye, well...just gonnae read something good. Yer losing the audience - this fella right here's away tae fall asleep', the old man replied, pointing right in his direction.

It was true. He had, despite the air of agitation pervading the room, let out a torpid and over-indulgent yawn, one which drew far too much attention to itself, and announced its presence with an unsubtle gesture of the shoulders that progressed through his entire torso. He looked to her. She seemed impassive, and was still very much focused on the speaker. He turned around and looked over to the little old man. 'Indeed, an accelerated praxis is something which is, at this historical moment, firmly within our grasp', the curator continued. The rest of the audience had now, too, apparently decided to completely ignore the interruption and had returned their attention to the front. A look of despondency came over the little old man's haggard face.

'Ah can see you Big Man...in wan ear and oot the other...but for a close mouth and aw that, I'll hud ma tongue. Just you tread carefully now.' He trudged over to the table and grabbed three bottles of beer, and clutched them close to his chest with one arm... and with the other waved a series of goodbyes – but nobody was watching him anymore as he shuffled quietly out of the door.

After the talk had finished, they hung around for a while – a few bottles of white wine had been brought out, and he drank two glasses. She had left him to his own devices while she wandered around and chatted to various groups of people congregating in different parts of the room. He felt awkward, and at that moment the thought of having to make any sort conversation filled him with dread. Instead, he pulled up a chair next to the window and watched her from afar. She moved seamlessly among the different groups, hugging people affectionately – or patting them softly on the shoulder whilst laughing sympathetically at their jokes. She approached one group which included the curator and three other older people who by their dress and manner seemed to have some importance. They reacted with instantaneous pleasure at her arrival, opening up their closed, conspiratorial circle – and allowing her twice the space required to accommodate her small frame. She launched into a monologue, replete with playful gestures dotted with a furrowing of her eyebrows when a serious point arose – all accompanied by that incandescent smile. Everyone reacted in just the right way, the only way that one would expect – with unqualified captivation and enthusiasm. After a while, she came back to where he was sitting.

'Ok let's head off, grumpy man. Let's go and get something to eat.' She said, pulling on his arm to lift him up from the seat.

He put his hands in his pocket and felt the foil of a blister pack. Inside was a red and black capsule which Robert had given him earlier. 'It's herbal, Chinese ah think…lasts for days.' He would give it a try, at least…there had to be a pharmacological way to surmount this problem, which was a very recent development after all, and one that could be explained away by alcohol…the brewer's droop. But deep down he knew that it was an affliction of the mind: an absence of hard thoughts inevitably led to soft results. It was a corporeal softness too – his body was in the process of becoming negligent, losing its firm edge; in his early teenage years he had been a promising footballer, a speed merchant, wiry, lean and with outsize height, the ability to hold the ball up and to finish when well placed - but at fourteen, this prospect was taken away by the Anterior Cruciate Ligament of his left knee, torn clean through by an overzealous slide tackle. When he was older he would lift weights regularly, and for a while it filled him out, increased his vascularity…but he lost interest after some time. 'It's better to take it on an empty stomach', Robert had said.

'There's a place just around the corner, I think, that does really good things, like really light – but it's so good, lots of garlic – which I might regret, but the noodles are so awesome – and its really really fresh too. Do you wanna go?'

'Of course.'

'Ok, let's go!'

She grabbed his arm and pulled him with a sudden jerk along the road. They walked down towards town for more than twenty-five minutes, around several corners, then headed further towards the west alongside the embankment. A slight fog skirted over the top of the river, and the streets were nearly empty. She was completely silent and leaned heavily onto his arm, and he could feel her trembling slightly even though it wasn't particularly cold, and she had on a thick black wool coat. He made some banal small talk but she didn't acknowledge it, looking back at him blankly – grinning faintly, almost catatonic.

'Is it nearby?' He asked.

'Nearby?'

'Near?' He asked.

'It's nearby.' She replied.

After a while he stopped asking questions. Eventually they crossed underneath the elevated carriageway and headed up towards Finnieston. They had been walking for almost an hour.

'That place.' She began, her voice trailing off slightly.

'Yeah?'

'That place is gone.'

'It's gone?'

It's not there anymore…it's no longer with us. But there's this other one, just along the road.'

'Ok, what's it called?' He asked.

'Oh…I can't remember – but it's so good. You'll love it.'

'But if you tell me what it's called I can maybe look up the directions?'

She didn't reply. They walked up past Anderston then came along the strip of Argyle Street past the junction. They were now only 5 minutes away from his flat. He regretted not tidying up, and wondered if Robert would be home. She wandered ahead of him and glanced into the different shop windows in a state of bewilderment and noticeable agitation. She quickened her pace and walked briskly along the street until she was almost fifty metres ahead of him, before stopping suddenly. She turned around and began waving both of her arms in the air, he jogged towards her and caught up – panting heavily, his brow slightly moist.

'It's here!'

'Oh ok…so it's this place, I've seen it before but I've never been inside – must be new. It changes around here quite a lot…'

'It's good…It's good…you'll see.'

The door to the restaurant was made of a weathered heavy wood, dark brown in colour – inside there were quite a number of people, but they only filled up around half of the large interior space which was over two floors. There were wood panels on the walls – the tables and parts of the bar were propped up by logs, all of a similar dark brown hue; the napkins, straws and glass lampshades were dark green, the lights around the marble topped tables, organised into rectangular booths with brown leather benches, were dim; a large mirror spanned the entire length of the bar, illuminated by bright lamps at its edges, and green bottles had been placed on the shelf underneath it – on each bottle there were white handwritten labels of the names of different liquors which had been decanted into them. He found a table near the corner and made a move to take her coat. She held up a hand and sat down. She still seemed to be shivering. She placed her handbag onto her lap and started rummaging around for something absentmindedly. He caught the attention of the waitress who started to make her way over to the table. She had stopped looking through her handbag and seemed to be fixated on the doorway.

'I haven't been here for a while' She replied, and at that moment she seemed almost on the point of tears.

'Is everything ok? You seem out of sorts.'

She didn't answer. The waitress approached and placed two menus on the table – she reached over and turned one of the menus to face her and weakly tried to flick it open with a limp wrist. The first couple of times it didn't stay open, but it worked on the third. Then, all of a sudden, as if gripped by a sudden burst of energy – she started flicking through the pages frantically.

'Can you bring me a gin and tonic.' She asked abruptly, not lifting her head up.

'What gin?'

'A double gin and tonic.'

'Sorry, I meant what kind of gin.'

'Dry gin.'

'We have three different kinds.'

'Surprise me. And get him a beer or something.'

'What…'

'I don't know doll, why don't you use a little imagination – just get him a beer.'

The waitress, a spindly and lanky girl of perhaps nineteen with a short auburn bob, blushed awkwardly and made a swallowing gesture with her mouth as she walked away. She picked up her handbag, stood up from the table brusquely and marched off towards the bathroom. The waitress came back with the drinks.

'I'm sorry, I don't think she's feeling well.' He said.

'Just give me a nod when you're ready to order.' The waitress replied.

There was a haunted aspect to this place; its glowing green bottles arranged with apothecary exactitude, the enchanted malice of the rough grainy wood, the dim lighting around the room, against the central eerie glow of the mirror – and the mausoleum cool of the black marble table tops. The waiting staff had a pallid look, slight, frail, underfed – they all seemed to express a comparable ungainliness in their motions and gestures. There was electronic music playing faintly but pervasively throughout the space, an amalgamation of ambient sounds and mixes of various non-descript house music. The place couldn't have been open for more than six months, and would no doubt close down within another six. She returned after ten minutes, smiling and serene. She took up her glass and drank half of its contents.

'I'm sorry.'

'Are you ok?'

'I'm fine…I had a really bad headache.'

'Shall I try and get you some painkillers?'

'No no, it's really ok now…I try not to take them anyway – they're really bad for your stomach. I think it's passed now. Anyway, yeah. The food is awesome here…I'm so excited! I want to order everything. I think I've pretty much tried all of the menu before, so I can tell you everything you wanna know.'

'Sure, but I'm not that hungry.'

'But…you have to eat something, what did you have for lunch?'

'A sandwich.'

'Oh that's nothing! Come on, you need to eat something more.'

'Ok.'

'Do you want me to order for you? God, I feel like your Mum.'

'Yeah, sure.'

'Ok darling, let's order you something with lots of vegetables.'

The waitress wandered back over cautiously. He reached into his pocket and popped the pill out of its blister pack and swallowed it discreetly.

'Hello, sorry about earlier – I was feeling a wee bit sick, but I'm alright now. He'll have the *Bún thịt nướng*, with extra bean sprouts – hey, they're really crispy and fresh, do you like them? I'll have them if you don't, I can totally eat them all day long – and then…I had a question actually. The Phat Thai with tofu thing, is that vegan?'

'Yeah, I think so.'

'Oh come on, pet. Is it vegan or not?' She snapped.

'It's vegan.'

'Great, thanks. I'll take that.'

The food was brought out within 5 minutes. His dish consisted of a congealed lump of glass noodles, a few pieces of pale fatty pork with a drizzle of some sort of brown sauce, garnished with 3 mint leaves, a slice of cucumber and a whole chilli pepper. More than half of the plate was covered in raw beansprouts, which, incidentally – he hated. He found that he was, in fact, very hungry. He picked up a piece of pork with his chopsticks and took a bite. It was completely cold and had a rubbery consistency. She glared at him from across the table, and then looked down at her own plate. She took a fork, stabbed one of the large lumps of fried tofu which was lying on top of her plate of noodles, brought it to her lips and shoved it into her mouth. She continued to glare at him while she chewed, a faint sense of disgust in her eyes as they filled up with tears. Suddenly, her body convulsed and made a choking sound. He leapt to his feet and made a move towards her – but she merely grabbed at the napkin to the side of her plate and spat out a half-digested piece of yellowy matter, now covered in her divine saliva. She then discreetly rolled up the napkin and placed it onto the table. Her red lipstick was smeared slightly on the left hand corner of her lip. She cleared her throat and took a sip of water. He sat back down.

'Shit, are you alright? I thought you were choking!'

'No, I'm fine – sorry. That's embarrassing.'

'You weren't choking?'

'No.' She looked down at her plate, and once again looked to be on the point of tears: 'This isn't vegan…they've used fish sauce.'

She took out a compact mirror and began reapplying her lipstick. In time, the waitress came over, mortified and remorseful. He felt a compulsion, rather acutely, that he should do all he could to fight her case in this regard. He looked over to her: she still seemed distraught. More of an expectation than a compulsion, perhaps. But looking over the awkward young waitress, and her evident resignation to the forthcoming ignoble reprimand from the petulantly tyrannical lackey who was probably her superior – he realised how unenviable his predicament was. What was the sense? Really. Perhaps he was a coward, but was it really such a big deal? He'd have to find out.

'I'm sorry, I didn't know that it wasn't vegan. We can bring another dish, and another round of drinks.' The waitress said.

'That's fine.' He replied. Perhaps this could be resolved amicably.

'I did ask.' She said, piping up weakly.

'Sorry?' the waitress replied.

'I asked if it was vegan. You said that it was. But it had fish sauce on it. I was almost very sick.' Her tone had all of sudden become menacingly deliberate and supercilious.

'Are you allergic?'

'No. I'm not allergic. But you should really pay more attention.'

'Can I bring you something else?'

'Yes, the bill.'

'Hey', he said enthusiastically, 'we can share mine – actually I really don't like beansprouts so you can have all of them, and really I just don't feel hungry at all.' It was true. He had lost his appetite.

'So, you're not going to eat anything?' She asked him with a pathetic expression. She then leaned across the table and picked up a few beansprouts with her fingers and chewed them sullenly. The slightly noticeable commotion at their table had drawn attention towards them, and a buzzing of grumbles and whispers rose steadily around them before dying down suddenly. From the upper floor a black silhouette descended, its long limbs gripping a silver tray – it stopped behind the bar and re-arranged some of the bottles, hovered around the tables and booths. He couldn't make out its face, but it was approaching steadily and lethargically. It approached closer. The half-greenish light now barely illuminated its face, the face of a man – whose own facial features were partially obscured by a beard, pitch black, bushy, but perfectly groomed. He wore a tight fitting black shirt with the sleeves rolled up to the elbows – and a brown leather apron which came down to his knees. There was a tattoo on the right hand side of his neck – a blindfolded woman holding a sword. On his right arm were the initials COC in solid black text. He arrived at their table and began speaking. 'Hi – I'm the manager, I just wanted to apologise about the mix-up.' The manager said. She continued re-applying her make-up without looking at up. He had let his eyes drift to the bar, where the waitress stood with a hand on her hip looking over to their table disdainfully. He became confused and disorientated.

'What mix-up?' He asked.

'The mix-up with your meal.' The manager replied.

'My meal was alright. The mix-up was with her meal.'

She put the mirror down, and turned to face the bearded manager. She gave him a hesitant look up and down, and began to smile.

'Brian. How long have you worked here?'

'I didn't notice it was you. We opened 6 months ago.'

'And how's it going? We were at a lovely talk and opening today – it was so interesting.'

'I heard about that. I wanted to go, but I had to work unfortunately.'

'How is your painting coming along?'

'Good. I moved into a bigger studio. My mate is on a residency for one year – so I took it off him. Lots of space, I'm happy with it.'

'That's terrific, I'll have to come around and see it some time. I'm really interested to see how the work has evolved.'

'You're always welcome' he replied. 'And you', Brian asked him abruptly. 'What do you do? Are you an artist?'

'Yes.'

'Oh, what kind?'

'A good one', he replied curtly.

'Ok then…So, I'm sorry again about the food. We have so many vegan options that it's difficult to keep track of them sometimes, and she's new. Our menu is always changing; we like to adapt it to the availability of local sustainable produce. Your meals and drinks are on the house.'

She giggled, and took a sip of her gin and tonic through the straw, and looked up to him smiling.

'Oh that's so sweet of you Brian, and I hope that the waitress err….'

'Clementine.'

'Clementine. What a lovely name! I really hope Clementine isn't too upset with me – I'm not feeling 100% today…I'm really worn out. You know how it is.'

'No worries. You should come to visit the studio, Clara. Have a nice evening guys.'

He let out a deep sigh and downed what was left of his beer. The food was mostly untouched but he longer felt in the mood to eat anything. She began staring off towards the entrance again.

'Who was that cunt?' he asked her.

'Just some wee guy I studied with. A painter. They're all over the place, these wee boys who paint big pictures with their big brushes.'

There was a bitterly cold wind blowing as they stepped out onto the empty street. He buttoned up his coat and started instinctively to walk towards home. Clara followed him and took his hand. They never spoke…he could feel his stomach rolling gently from side to side. As he was opening the door to the close, he felt a stabbing pain – a pain more severe than any he had ever felt before behind his eyes, alternating between each temple. It almost blinded him, and he was scarcely able to see the keyhole. He turned to her, and could make out the pale white outline of her face but her nose, her lips, and eyes were all covered by a fuzzy static, as if the pixels of which they were composed had been lost in communication – present but indistinct. She asked him if he was ok. He replied that he was. He managed to eventually open the door and thankfully the pain started to subside. They were alone in the flat, it seemed – but he quickly ushered her into the bedroom just in case Robert came home. The bed was unmade, and the duvet was still without a cover – the curtains were drawn in the room and it was completely dark. The lightbulb went out with a sharp popping sound as he switched it on, and he wandered into the kitchen to look for another. There was a note on the fridge saying that Robert had gone away, and to take his washing out the machine. He led her into the living room, which was permeated by a hollow and rancorous chill. Clara sat down on the couch and took off her coat. He went to turn the heating on and remembered the time when they had both moved in here, and hadn't ever put it on during the winter. They would walk around fully dressed with their bathrobes over their clothes – using tea-lights on a plate with a plant pot over the top, drinking endless pints of tea from beer mugs. He was just as miserable then, but somehow it seemed preferable to be in that moment as opposed to the present one. To pick at an old wound. Clara didn't seem to feel the cold. He brought over a bottle of wine and opened it. The pain behind his eyes and at his temples had lessened, but it was still there – a stubborn ache which made it difficult for him to think. He needed to think, because he hadn't said anything for the entire time that she had been there. She hadn't spoken either. The air had already become stale and oppressive with all of the things left unsaid. He had wanted nothing more than to see here again for these past few days, but now that she was in front of him - leaning back unconvincingly against the couch and staring awkwardly at him and towards the floor – her presence was almost unwelcome. He had run out of ideas, so he opted instead to look into her eyes in the hopes that this would suffice in keeping her occupied. She noticed his gaze, but averted it – shuffling uncomfortably in her seat and pulling at a thread that was hanging loose at the bottom of her jumper. She was nervous. He looked out of the window – the scenery was unmoving, an eerie stillness prevailed. The thought of her being nervous brought back a short jolt of that evening's previous panic. He poured out two glasses of wine, and drank at his own a little too rapidly. He was thinking too much. He wanted to kiss her, but the process by which he would arrive at that particular point was muddled in his brain. He took another long drink of his wine, and wandered over to the speakers and plugged in his phone. She got up and headed towards the bathroom, closing the door behind her. He let it play on shuffle; the first song he skipped, too rasping and scratchy, the expression of another mood entirely – the second he skipped as well, and had no idea what it was even doing on his playlist – the third was *April Skies*. For all intents and purposes the skies were always April…no need to be reminded of it…he left it on in any case. He felt himself becoming warm and clammy, and the rolling in his stomach started up again. He got up and headed towards the kitchen, closing the door behind him. He stood in the kitchen for a few moments, but realised there was no reason for him to be there – so he headed back. When he opened the door to the living room, she was standing right in front of him and they almost bumped into one another.

'We shouldn't listen to this song', she said, looking at him with a startled and worried look.

'Why?'

'Because it gives me the shivers…and its already really cold in here.' He pulled her gently towards him by the waist, and she reached up and put her arms around his neck.

…

This realisation, it came all of a sudden, and I put those headphones in and I was almost on the point of tears you know? No, I was crying, I was bubbling, bawling – and the music, it formed into a crescendo, and I was walking in the midst of that sweating mass, their hideous faces and appetites, and what is a man if not an appetite, his first and his last; and it was all so ugly, so trifling and pointless but none so pointless as myself, who had only wanted to live…but either/or, impossible to do both – paralysis is the logical conclusion of attempting an untruth – but nothing when compared to the general logic of crisis, and its assemblages of malcontent. Masses of assembly. Then in assembly mass. Good optics. He can come up, that wee lad, and light a candle or whatever beside this wee Buddha or…there you go…ecumenical…that would be an ecumenical matter wouldn't it, father? Felt like a right fanny, lighting a candle to some wee bald cunt he knows nothing about- seeing as I'm a pape just like the rest of youse cunts. I'm a tarrier, a taig, a Fenian. I wis on the *Rue d'Ulm*, giving the missus a relaxing a wee neck message after a hard day's....shagging? Unlikely. That isn't a woman, that's a waterfall...He could hear the steady rising and falling of her breath next to him – it seemed to become louder with each intake and exhale until it filled the room entirely, bouncing off the walls and making the windows tremble - louder, then louder still, until he was on the banks of a wide and powerful cascade, the pounding of its gushing torrents cancelled out all of the other noise in the room – he could no longer hear his own heartbeat, and thought that maybe it had stopped. He jumped out of the bed, and smashed his knee against the drawer of the bedside table, which had been pulled out. She stirred in her sleep and moaned, rolled onto her back and muttered incoherently. He rummaged around in the drawer but he couldn't find them; he ran to the bathroom, searched through the cabinet and found the small card Xanax box – but inside there were only three empty blister packs. He peered down into the bottom of the box where a couple of minute clumps and some powdery pink dust had gathered – he poured it out onto his palm and desperately licked the stale bitter remnants. He headed back into the room and got into bed. All at once the room seemed altogether too large, the ceilings too high – the walls too wide; it's now vast interior existing only to emphasise his miniscule body, its fragility and its increasing peril. He began to shake violently and was breathing loudly and rapidly with a rasping pant, like a sickly dog which had over-exerted himself. He could feel droplets of sweat forming on his forehead, and reached up to wipe his brow – his hand covered in a warm sticky moisture. She sat up in bed with a start.

'What's the matter?' She asked, breathlessly. But he was unable to speak.

...

In the morning when he awoke, Clara was lying on top of him. Already dressed but without make-up – she was resting her chin on his chest and staring at him inquisitively. There was a sharp pain at each of his temples and a powdery dryness at the back of the throat. He sleepily surveyed her face, and its expression, which at that moment without its layers of expert shading and contouring had a look of remote bewilderment – the faint dark circles and lines of her eyelids, and the eyes themselves – less prominent, more subdued, bestowed on her a fatigued and pitiable aspect, which contrasted to her sprightly mood. She asked him something, but he wasn't awake enough yet to tell what it was. It wasn't a face that he had seen before, and he felt vaguely that he was in the presence of a stranger, but one whose company was somehow preferable to the woman from the previous night. She turned her head to the side and read the book she had lifted off the bedside table. He remembered seeing an entirely different face the previous night, gazing up towards it from between her soft white thighs, wet to the touch - staring down as she then took his cock into her surprisingly dry mouth….and then the crestfallen look of a sympathy that bordered on scorn, as it stubbornly refused to fulfil its primary function. He groaned loudly. She rolled off the bed and headed out of the room, coming back after five minutes with a cup of black coffee.

'You're out of sugar. I just met your flatmate.'
'I don't take sugar.'
'Does it make you nervous?'
'…'
'Can I make you some toast?'
'I don't usually eat breakfast.'
'Ugh….that's not good at all is it?

She placed her cup onto the bedside table and picked up the book again, flicking through the pages and stopping at where he had dog-eared the page.

'Do you do that with all your books? Why don't you just use a bookmark?'

'I dunno. Books are tools, there's no need to be precious with them.'

'Your body, I shall cherish and love, as a soldier, amputated by war, unwanted and friendless, cherishes his last remaining leg.'

'Yes.'

'That's cheery.'

He sat up on the bed, rubbed his eyes and yawned. She stared at him. His leg shook slightly. She came over and sat beside him on the bed.

'Gimme your hand.' She took his left hand by the wrist and reached into the pocket of her jeans. She pulled out a thin light blue hair bobble and put it on his wrist.

'Whenever you feel like that again, just do this….' She pulled the elastic of the hairband until there was no more give and snapped it back, causing him to flinch with pain. She bowed down and kissed his hand.

'I need to go, I have some things to do.'

'Can't you stay for a little bit?'

'I'm sorry, I can't. You should go out and do something – it's a lovely day!'

After he heard the front door click as she left, he got dressed and headed into the bathroom where he washed his face briefly and brushed his teeth hurriedly. He headed back into the bedroom and got dressed. The door to his bedroom was slightly ajar, and he caught a glimpse of Robert busying himself with something at his window – he knocked on the door and went in.

'Oh, hud on a minute. There he is…shagger.'

At the window there was a battered easel made of old and slightly rotting wood – on it he had a canvas which he was attacking enthusiastically with a medium sized brush. For thirty seconds at a time he would lunge and thrust at it with his right hand, breathing heavily and grunting slightly – then step back to observe. The left hand he kept in the back pocket of his jeans.

'Where were you yesterday?'

'Eh? I went to Mugdock Park, walked around a bit – and I went to see ma Da in Clydebank, got a bit steaming so I crashed.'

'Well?'

'What?'

'Is that where the inspiration came from, a brief wee walk in a park barely outside the city limits…contemplating nature – taking in some picturesque scenery…To stroll among our trees and stray in Goosegog Lane'

'Not quite, no.'

Robert took three steps back, and stood to the side. So far, there were four colours that jostled for attention from the boundaries, a yellowish beige, a dark grey, an off-white and black. Other than this, the most prominent was a subdued and pale pink. On first glance, it was difficult to detect a pattern – but something seemed to be there within this array of shapes, both angular and curving, with sharp and soft edges. He looked at it for some time. Robert rolled a cigarette and lit it. Eventually something began to emerge, something corporeal amid that calculated mess of powdery wet paint. Robert opened up his laptop. On the screen was a video, paused on an image of a beautiful woman's face. The face was clear and distinct amid the blurred edges, the perspective seemed to come from above, and from the left, she looked over her right shoulder, which was bare. Even from the first glimpse it was affecting, but as you lingered longer it was possible to recognise a countenance which was immediate – an assertive judgement, devoid of cruelty, which saturated the entire screen. The sum of all of this was a sentiment, one he could not quite place, but the existence of which he found impossible to deny; and nor could anyone who had once learned, only to somehow forget, the fevered waves and subtle ripples of its eternal and mysterious language. He felt his knees shaking weakly and awkwardly sat down on the corner of the bed – never taking his eyes from the screen. Robert smiled.

'Exactly. I found this last night.' He loudly tapped the spacebar.

The camera jerked and zoomed out slowly but steadily, she bobbed her head – turned her head away, then looked back at the camera, her face by now contorted into a sultry grimace – and then a laugh, different now, as she rounded her mouth and moaned as she rode roughshod on top of that anonymous cock, a pair of hairy hands with gold signet rings pulling apart her glistening oily buttocks, a finger teasing the edges of her gushing wet cunt. She moaned and laughed, and licked her lips with her pale pink tongue to a background cacophony of grunts and words of moronic and obscene encouragement. Robert tapped the spacebar again.

'I've been looking for this.'

'What ye on about mate? Why you showing me yer wanking material?'

'Right, just forget about that for a second. You noticed it as well.'

'Noticed what?'

'It was there, I saw it, and you saw it. You can't deny it. It still exists, and I intend to capture it.'

'What is it, exactly?'

'Come on, there's no need to spell it out.'

'Ok I did see it. I saw it for a second. But then it was gone.'

'Why?'

'Because it's been sullied…cheapened, somehow, made mundane and everyday. When it becomes those things, it no longer exists.'

'I don't agree. Maybe I thought like that too, but then – there it was, at 3am, half-pished in your childhood bedroom, a jittery stream on a shaky wifi connection.'

'You're delusional if you believe that.'

'Maybe I am…here listen; you have to play the cards you're dealt – find your Giacondas in the rubbish heap of desire; no use waiting for some seismic shift that'll probably never come.'

'Have you been looking for it specifically, in amongst this?'

'Gotta get in amongst it, ma man. I always suspected that it was possible…but yeah, in a way. We spend enough time wanking as it is, might as well combine it with something useful eh?'

'Awrite, nae danger. So it was research then, the other night…'

'What you oan about?'

'Nah, doesn't matter.'

'So what's happening wi this bird?'

'What dy'a mean?'

'I mean, what's the score?'

'Dunno, dunno. I really like her…but there's an issue.'

'What kind of issue?'

'An issue.'

'I see.'

'It's an issue with my perception, I'm sure it is.'

'Does she like you? I mean, does she really like you?'

'No idea.'

'Hud on a minute. Perception, what d'ya mean by that?'

'It's difficult to know what she's thinking.'

'That's not particularly surprising….given that she's a woman'

'But I need to know.'

'Why d'ya you need to know?'

'Otherwise, what's the point…there has to be an ending.'

'You want it tae proceed along a pre-determined path, where's the fun in that? There's always an ending. The ending is: you'll be dead, eventually.'

'That's a second ending. A different ending. I'm interested in the first. But I don't think so…there's something there, I know it – I just need a clear view. I need to know what's gonna happen. Or, no, I just need to know what she's feeling – I need to know. I can't get my head off the ground, or calm down– or do anything, otherwise'

'You need to know because it's more comforting and familiar if things are predictable.'

'Now what are *you* oan about?'

'You want this to be like the others. You want to mimic it, to parrot it, to modify it slightly – but essentially to have it be just the same. I already told you how it'll go: exactly how it's gone before. So, what do think is different about her?'

'…honestly, I dunno.'

'Guess I'm no the only delusional cunt round here.'

'…'

'Anyway. What do you know about ritual sacrifice?'

'Not interested in talking about religion mate, not now.'

'Nah I mean…when they actually just topped cunts to please a God or gods or summat– cut their throat on alters or threw them in a volcano or something like that. Been reading about it.'

'What's this go tae do wi it?'

'Nothing really, or I dunno maybe something. I'm just tryna to change the subject. Get a wee break from you moaning about yer shite.'

125

'Tell me.'

'The person they want to sacrifice has to be innocent, or if they sacrifice an animal – it has to be one of the nice, kind animals – the docile, friendly ones. Pets essentially. None of yer hyenas, wolves and tigers. Anyway…from what I understand, they need to be innocent because their sacrifice is a payment for some form of debt or guilt committed by society. It's a highly moral affair, inntit.'

'Disnae seem like a good deal for the victim.'

'They weren't victims. Many of them chose to be killed.'

'Still…I think your understanding isn't really complete."

'How?'

'There's nothing moral that I can see.'

'Go on then…"

'Right, so I can accept that the victim must be perceived to be innocent, and maybe they're indifferent to their own fate… and even chose it. They choose the victims, or the victims choose themselves, because their supposed innocence is in fact naivety – an inability to adopt to the comprehensive corruption of society. This society wants tae protect itself, as flawed and corrupt as it is – there's violence all around them, but none of them wanna be killed going about their daily grind of bullshit by some random cunt. But at the same time, they need to see violence done, because they themselves are fundamentally embroiled in violence and are capable of imagining its immediate form, but not its consequences. They need it, they're bloodthirsty but at the same time squeamish. So they get this hapless cunt, convince him he's doing some divine duty – treat him well, and then….'

'They kill him.'

'Exactly.'

'Awrite, whatever….god it's no always all about you all the time mate. Here, let's go for a walk or something. I need a break. What's the weather like?'

'Looks alright.'

He sauntered into his bedroom and dug around the wardrobe, which had very few clean warm clothes – aside from a green woollen jumper. Barely worn, it had been an unwanted Christmas present from an auntie some years ago. He hesitated, but finding nothing else, he grabbed the jumper from its coat hanger and hurriedly put it on. It was dry when they got out onto the street, but the faint chill of the wind and the metallic taste of the moist air suggested the imminent onset of rain – but they began walking anyway, shoulders hunched and hands in pockets, talking loudly, crossing the park and the museum, then across the bridge towards Partick before doubling back and meandering around the rear of Kelvinhall, and then up near Yorkhill – towards the direction of home. Robert seemed to be in good spirits, joking nonstop and laughing vigorously at his own jokes, which were mostly at other people's expense – he maintained his mood even when he talked about things that were, in essence, less than positive recent developments such as his potential upcoming redundancy, and his father's worsening emphysema. Nothing seemed to come near him, nothing could touch him. Everything which was occurring to him at that point in time or even to others close to him seemed detached from his current mood – a mood of inspiration and accomplishment. It was infuriating. Without agreement, they stopped walking. Robert took out his tobacco and rolled a cigarette. He held out the pack to him with a nod of the head.

'Maybe shouldn't.'

'You trying tae quit?'

'I should try to…here, by the way, the pill you gave me didn't work. Just gave me a headache.'

'Gutted.'

'Aye.'

'But it's nothing to dae wi those pills…they're fucking brand new.'

'How?'

'Mate, it's yer heid.'

A brief glimpse of a particular scene flashed before his eyes, half soaked in the icy glow of a sedate moonlight which was interrupted in places by the punitive orange glimmering of the streetlamps… it was his head, hyperventilating, gasping for breath, with tears streaming down his face – and then the scene becomes indistinct… all that was left were the sensations, the touch of her cold fingers as his head was pulled towards the softness of her breast and held there, rocked gently backwards and forwards, and the feeling of fingers running through his hair. She was gently humming that song, the song she hummed in the bar that first night. The song, he now knew, was *April Skies*.

They stood at that street corner, between Argyle and Radnor Street. The monotonous thumping of a bass drum, at first muffled, could be heard making an approach, followed on all sides of its centralised beat by the rolling of snares – it came from their left, and became louder, then louder still, followed by the tinny metallic rasp of whistles and flutes. The crowd was upon them. Meaty unsmiling policeman at its head and at its sides - looking askance in all directions, followed by old men in black suits, orange sashes and bowler hats, wrinkled and weathered red faces strained through inarticulate caterwauling – waving umbrellas and large walking sticks, some barely limping along…behind them were other, younger men, drifting in lazy formation, men with banners, men with flags, a line of drummers in blue attempting to keep a steady roll, punctuated by the out of sync hammering of big bass drums beaten with increasing violence…in and around them - or behind, it was difficult to tell – were lines of more men with whistles and flutes, their cheeks inflating and deflating with a passionate fury and determination to add their shrill wailing screeches to that tumult…suddenly the crowd didn't seem to have an end, the crowd seemed to move off in all directions, forwards, backwards, diagonally, pointing upwards towards the grey indifferent skies, and back down onto the unforgiving tarmac; the crowd contained everyone and everything…the mass of the crowd drifted past other crowds – crowds of bemusement, curiosity, and fear at its side-lines – some appearing from their window sills above the street, in t-shirts and vests, rubbing their bleary eyes, yawning through cursing expressions. A line of children, boys and girls in red uniforms, their eyes downcast, blew meekly into their little flutes, struggling to keep in step, occasionally falling behind, then running to catch up…men, and more men, and then some groups of women in black dresses and oranges sashes – men with white uniforms, men in grey uniforms and blue hats, some in dark blue. The crowd was interminable, its mass all encompassing. The throng of the crowd crept up the street, and as it progressed it lost its form, the half ordered lines and uniforms gave way to another horde, more amorphous, disgorging itself onto the pavements, a motley assortment of dress; jeans, t-shirts in spite of the cold wind, in innumerable shades of blue – windbreakers, parkas, puffy coats adorned with compasses on the sleeve, not a uniform but adhering to a certain semiotic code nonetheless; they were draped in Union flags, bloated and puckered flesh – weather-beaten, psoriatic, thrusting their fists in the air, screaming at the top of their lungs, their voices breaking under the strain of exaggerated sentiments,

– the air swiftly became thick with the aroma of over-indulgence and bile. The crowd would never end, and it would be impossible to escape. The crowd was whipping itself up into a frenzy, prowling defiantly, searching desperately for something, breaking in the middle, then reforming thicker than before – more police attempt to herd the crowd along, to control the flowing swarm of malignity but could do nothing more than observe, and in any case seemed apathetic…lumps of crowd here and there attempt to break off, some become disorientated and stumble in circles, but eventually find their bearing and resume their forward march. And he felt the momentary urge, despite it all, to join them – to join the crowd. A shatter of breaking glass echoed. The drums, though further afield, seemed to grow louder, their arrhythmic tribal thumping only growing more substantial, more menacing, more defiant, until all of the noises, the sensations, the smells and shouts seemed to explode, amplifying and merging into one overpowering, deafening and monstrous roar. And then everything stopped. He looked at Robert who was smoking his cigarette, wide-eyed and with a stupid mocking grin plastered onto his face. The crowd had stopped marching. Looking way down the road, a police van could be seen holding up the march. Mutterings, grumblings, and muted laughter amongst the crowd – they looked around at each other. A cracking in the grey firmament, an ominous rumble – then the instantaneous deluge…thick globules of cold rain pummelled the crowd, soaking them through and rattling the pavement – the march started up again, the crowd, with less enthusiasm now, more muted, more sombre, its spirits dampened, but its pyretic energy still intact, trudged onwards. Eventually it began to thin out, the last few of the crowd, the stragglers stumbled and staggered along the road. Once the crowd had almost passed, the reverberations of panic welled up inside him. He dug his fingers into his palms and looked around suspiciously. He exhaled deeply.

'You alright? Looking a bit flustered there, chief.' Robert asked.

'Aye, I'm fine.' He replied, attempting a laugh.

He waited for Robert to look away, and snapped the blue hair bobble onto his wrist – the short sharp sting leaving a reddish indentation. His phone vibrated in his pocket and he pulled it out. 'Are you feeling ok? xxx.' The panic receded, but in its place was a steadily simmering anger. A figure, among the last of the crowd, stumbled purposefully towards him – a rotund mass of sinew and ground meat, bulging at the belly, his shiny bald head glistening with raindrops. The eyes were bloodshot and yellow, contorted and intimidating. The figure approached and stood looming over him – twice his own width – muttering rambling insults and stabbing a hairy pudgy finger repeatedly into his chest, then shoving him with increasing force. Another two stragglers were approaching behind, heading in his direction. He looked around at Robert, who pulled his t-shirt with his finger tips and nodded towards his green jumper. In one fluid motion, he turned around and threw his forehead forward with all of his weight onto the bridge of the man's broad orange peel nose – feeling the crack on impact. His adversary stumbled to the side. Almost immediately, he felt the full impact of a right hook from one of the others land on the left hand side of his face – almost knocking him clean off his feet. He fell to the ground. A buzzing numbness filled his head. Robert jumped in, throwing a few wild punches, none making contact, and receiving one in return – until four coppers rushed over and broke them up. He struggled to his feet. A continuous beeping sound filled his ears. One of the policeman looked them over, snarling through gritted teeth: 'Get outta here! Go home!'

They stumbled along the short distance back to their flat on the now empty and crowd-less street, holding each other up. They could barely contain their laughter the entire way.

...

He walked into the bedroom and threw his coat onto the chair – but it landed with half of its weight hanging over onto the side, before slowly sliding down onto the floor with a hissing sound. From the bag he took out a flat white packet wrapped in shiny transparent plastic film, which he tore off – removing the pristine white duvet covers and throwing the cardboard backing and plastic clips into the bin. He brought the stiff white sheets to his face and breathed in their chemical freshness. Coming home from work at the bar a little past midnight, he had gone straight to bed – sleeping only for a few hours. He came around at a little past 5 am, and unable to go back to sleep completely, he found himself lying half-dazed, on the frontier of a diaphanous bluish dawn. As much as he had willed it, she would not appear whole – unravelled and untangled – in his frenzied dreams, among the snippets of half-remembered conversations and variegated visions, which the relentless onslaught of passing years had tied into an enormous yarn of multifarious wool - coveted from behind the blurry glass of a shop window display. Only momentary sightings, shadows, spectres which never became substantial; sensations and objects which merely hinted at her presence – and situations in which she should have figured, but where her absence was keenly felt. It was only upon waking, in those first few moments of blissful half-sleep, that she would take form in his thoughts – sending silent waves of jagged electricity through every nerve fibre. And for those all too brief moments he felt the giddy nausea of anticipation, the delirious thrill of being alive, which would last no longer than the few minutes it took for him to wake up entirely. When he awoke that morning, he was faced with a realisation: that the threads were slipping from his grasp, and that they had already begun to fall to the ground in knots. He understood, all at once, that without her, even those few moments of azure dawn would disappear entirely, and with them the last remnants of sanity, and any hope of reaching those distant shores beyond. He leapt out of bed.

Throughout the day he set about tidying the entire flat; clearing out various debris…gathering up all of the half-drunk cups of tea with pieces of pale green mould floating on the surface, the glasses of stagnant water – crumbs of rolling tobacco, filters, papers, boxes, tissues, newspapers; he hoovered for three hours, washed stains from the carpets, wiped down all of the surfaces in the bathroom and kitchen with bleach, washed every plate, cup and glass, dried them, and put them back into the cupboards. He did basket after basket of washing. All of the windows of the flat were cleaned, and were now open; outside the air was crisp and cool, and the sun was shining. He went into town and bought some new sheets. When he returned, it was early afternoon. He held each corner of the top of the duvet and placed them into the unbuttoned cover, and, adhering to that childhood habit, climbed in, slotted each corner to the top of the cover, and lingered inside the warm sterile blankness before eventually emerging again. He then took the bottom corners and held them in place – flapping the duvet three times as if spreading out a tablecloth. He sat down on the bed and felt the tender bruises underneath his blackened left eye, and slowly ran his fingers across the bottom lip – cautiously probing the protruding cut on its left-hand side, and the dried blood that was still slightly moist to the touch.

He stood up quickly and felt the rush to his head temporarily blurring his vision and making him light-headed. He removed his t-shirt and walked into the living room. Earlier on, when tidying up, he had dug out a weights bench and a dusty box filled with an assortment of black iron weights and bars which he set up in the livingroom. He lay down on the bench, gripped onto the cold steel barbell and began his reps. It was much less weight than he had once been accustomed to. He gritted his teeth and strained, his arms and chest burned and throbbed – he grunted and panted, pushed up, and pulled down, until failure, and then carefully placed the barbell onto the clips when had finished. He stood up and grabbed the dumbbells, and patiently and methodically made his way through several sets of various lifts; lateral raises, curls, hammer curls, preacher curls and rows. He fell back onto the couch, covered in a film of sticky sweat – winded and buzzing. He squeezed his engorged arms, closed his eyes and fell in step with the pulsating flow making its way through the tributaries of veins and sinuous tissue. It soothed him to feel it welling up in him; a purifying energy, a clarity, a life-force; he felt himself drifting off to sleep. When he awoke, it was still as sunny as before – but the sun had shifted along. There was a ringing at the doorbell, at first in short rapid bursts, which then became longer – until a continuous buzzing filled the entire flat. He got up from the sofa, groggy and befuddled, and drifted lethargically towards the door.

'Hi! Can I come in?'

Clara stood in front of him. She was breathing heavily, and her hair was down at her shoulders – a voluminous brown mane, with kinks and frizz, blown out in all directions by the wind, framed her face. There was a thin layer of perspiration on her forehead; her mascara was running slightly underneath her eyelids. She wore a light blue t-shirt, tight grey jeans and a black leather jacket with the sleeves rolled up above the wrists.

'I ran all the way here. Just let me catch my breath.' She bent her head forward and continued panting exaggeratedly. She started laughing to herself.

'From where?' He asked.

'Oh, erm, yeah, I dunno.'

'Is there something wrong?'

'No, nothing. I just wanted to see you.'

'I was sleeping.'

'Oh, I'm sorry…did I wake you? Tough shit, I'm coming in anyway.' She replied pushing past him, running her cold fingers over his bare chest as she passed. 'Could I have a glass of water? That's the kitchen right? Ok, where's the glasses again?' She kicked off her shoes in the hallway, and walked around the kitchen quickly and agitatedly, throwing open cupboards and closing them until she arrived at the one with glass tumblers on the top shelf. She stood up on her tiptoes and reached both of her hands up, trying to edge the nearest glass closer to her hand with her fingertips: 'I need to grow a couple more inches!' She then climbed onto the kitchen top – one knee at a time – and the stood up on the counter. She picked out two glasses. 'Right, how do I get down?' He walked over to her, placed his arms on the back of her thighs and lifted her slowly from the counter – he loosened his grip, and she gradually slid down onto the floor. She ran the cold water full blast and drank two glasses, filled it again – and then offered it to him. He took a sip and placed it on the counter. He still tasted sleep in his mouth. She looked at him, screwed up her face and wrinkled her nose.

'Can you like, put on a t-shirt or something?'

He made a move to turn and leave the kitchen, but as he was doing so – she threw her arms around him from behind and lightly dug her nails into his chest. 'God, I wasn't being serious! Let's go to the living room.' She led him by the hand to the living room and pushed him down onto the sofa. She gathered her loose hair behind her head and made as if to tie it into a pony tail – but simply held it between her fingertips before letting it fall back down. She pulled off her jacket, swung it above her head and then threw it onto the armchair. She climbed on top of him and began covering his mouth with a barrage of frantic wet kisses, sticking her tongue down his throat and digging her nails into his arms, emitting low moans. She stopped kissing him suddenly and moved her head back, placing a hand underneath his chin and examining him.

'Shit, what happened to your face?'

'I got punched.'

'Why?'

'I think it was an aesthetic disagreement.' He replied.

'Ok, stop talking rubbish. Why are you going around getting into fights?' She added, assuming a combative expression.

'I couldn't really do anything about it. It just happened.'

'So did you provoke it, or were you attacked?'

'It's difficult to say.'

'Why?'

'It happened quickly.'

'When?'

'It doesn't matter, it's stupid. Forget it.'

'I know it's stupid. God!'

She climbed off him, got to her feet, stretched out her arms and began pacing around the living room, back and forth, her hand on her waist, focusing on the floor and looking up at him occasionally – she then stopped, walked over to the open windows and shut them. She placed her hand back onto her hip and started pacing again. 'This type of violence is so primitive and atavistic, I know it's stupid, it's stupid…violence is stupid…the violent are stupid. Its degenerate, base stupidity. And what, what am I supposed to think about it? Am I supposed to be impressed or something? Oh, it doesn't bother me….I'll leave the violent to it…leave them to their violence. But…ugh' She looks up at him and bites her bottom lip, takes a bobble from somewhere in her pocket and tied her hair up in a ponytail, before storming out of the room and slamming the door. She walked back in a moment later, holding his t-shirt, and roughly wrapped around his head. 'Put that on, it's cold in here… you'll catch a chill. I'm hungry now…like really hungry…what did you have to eat for lunch?' He put his arms through the sleeves and pulled the t-shirt on.

'I made some soup…lentil soup. Do you wanna have some?'

'Really? Oh wow. I love lentil soup! But let's go and do something now, the sun's shining and the weather's so lovely today. Let's go and sit in the park, or go and feed the squirrels – or I dunno….bowls. Oh, let's play lawn bowls!' She walked over to him and lifted his chin upwards with her hand. Tears began to fill her eyes. 'That's so horrible…I'm so sorry…does it hurt?' she asked breathlessly.

'It's fine…can you just sit down for a minute.' He asked her, guiding her onto the couch next to him.

'Is there something wrong?' He asked, sternly. She composed herself instantly.

'No…I'm fine.' She got back up and took her handbag from the coffee table and left the room again, closing the door behind her quietly. He heard the bathroom door click closed. She came back two minutes later, looking subdued, with a happy sadness in her eyes.

'Ok bruiser…let's go and play.'

They left the flat, turned left, walked down to the bottom of the road, and entered the bowling green. The sky glowed red and deep orange. Another group of players were finishing up their game and preparing to leave. He knocked on the pavilion door and a chubby, ruddy-cheeked old man opened the door and, without a word, handed them a basket containing a jack and a set of bowls. They picked a rink near to the road, next to a bench, from which you could see people wandering lazily in and out of the park along Gray street – the clouds, with a soft down of pink fluff, seemed to mimic the motion of the people below, indolently making their way across the sky. A passing breeze brought a chill, and she zipped up her jacket and folded her arms. She began to look around, a little bored, and then towards him. He rolled the jack down the green. He walked down towards it, picked it up and centred it. He thought of that first night, when he had seen her on the stage, obscured and blurry – and then again, when she sat down in front of him. For a brief moment, an infinitesimal second, before they had even spoke, he felt that he already knew everything that there was to know about her, that even her name – which he didn't yet know – was already familiar to him, but with each passing remark and enquiry, this raw certainty became shrouded in a cold miasma of indeterminacy. She sat down on the bench, crossed her legs, took a long thin cigarette out of her packet by pulling it with her teeth, and lit it. She took a deep, long drag and blew the smoke upward towards the sky.

'You go first.' She said.

He picked up a bowl and rolled it with a little too much force. It advanced rapidly down the green, curving completely around the jack at a safe distance, before landing in the trench with a dry thud. He swore under his breath. She looked up towards him with her mouth open in an expression of faux-shock. She sprung up from the bench, cigarette clenched between her teeth, picked up a bowl nonchalantly, and kneeling down, she rolled it onto the green with a precise and measured motion of her right hand; the bowl moved gracefully downward along the green, mapping out a satisfyingly curved trajectory, the brown indentations on its surface moving in harmonious, rhythmical pattern as it approached the jack steadily, eventually coming to a halt no more than two centimetres away from it. She turned to him, smirked and walked slowly back to the bench. He stood there watching her, studying her every movement, the tightening of the skin on the back of her long tender neck, her supple hips with their almost unnoticeable swing, the way her feet fell onto and lifted themselves from the ground, the slight roll of her taught thighs as they contracted and relaxed. Something fell from her grasp, a red plastic lighter, and landed with a brittle impact onto the gravel beside the bench. She bent down to pick it up revealing a fleeting glimpse of white lace just below the mole on the small of her back. She sat back down and finished her cigarette. He couldn't help staring at her, never lingering too long before training his eyes onto the green, the road, or off into the distance – he felt that she was aware of every stolen glance, and that her gestures, her movements and expressions were seemingly made in full awareness of the enchanting effect that she was having upon him. She was watching him, watching her.

She slipped out of his embrace and stood up slowly from the bed, drawing the curtains with ceremonial precision and leaving a generous gap, which filled the now darkened room with the burnt yellow glow of the setting sun. She turned to him, untied her hair, removed her t-shirt and jeans, unclipped her bra and threw it onto the bed. The wide beam of late afternoon sunlight shone a spotlight onto her hair, and the central tranche of her torso. Her dark hair, now light and fair, mixed with the intrusive sunlight. He took off his trousers and t-shirt beneath the covers, got up from the bed and slowly made his way to where she was standing and put his arm around her waist – she took his face in her hands, pulled it towards her own and kissed his mouth. He lifted her up and laid her on the bed, peeled off her white lace underwear, gently pried open her thighs and buried his face between them – his tongue making slow lingering rotations around the top of her cunt. She began to moan slowly, and he felt the goosebumped skin of her inner thighs close around his ears – every so often a jolt would cascade through her body, and she would convulse, pushing down further onto his open mouth. She tapped him on the head, and he surfaced. She looked indulgently into his eyes, burning a hole right through his forehead – his cock was so stiff that its bulging head felt as if it would burst off from its shaft.

 He directed his gaze towards the box of condoms at the bedside table, and she turned her head to follow his line of sight – then turned back to him, sat up and pulled him towards her. They kept their eyes locked on one another as he entered into her and propelled himself forward slowly, before retreating, then advancing again. Her stare was relentless, all-encompassing, possessed of a feverish intensity that seemed to contain within it a judgement, an expectation, an obligation, a promise, and a duty that he felt incapable of ever honouring. He became instantaneously distracted at this sudden flaring forth of her preternatural beauty. He felt himself losing his erection with each thrust, and averted her heated gaze. He pulled out, place both his hands on either side of her waist, lifted her up and flipped her over – taking a moment to ingrain the image onto his mind, before entering into her again. He held her tight by the waist, and as he thrust with increasing power he felt his errant cock regain its previous vigour. She began groaning louder, then louder – he ran his hands along her waist and squeezed her breasts in his palms, then felt down along her ribcage and back onto her arse, squeezing it tightly as he quickened the pace and force of his thrusts – the room was filled with deafening screams of pleasure, which gushed forth from her mouth in a torrent of language, of the transcendent sounds and expletives of which such poetry is composed, until he could suddenly feel her legs shaking, then her entire body, and then the screams reached a crescendo: he pulled out his cock, spurting onto her back. She collapsed onto the bed, and he lay down beside her. She buried her face in the pillow, and it emerged periodically, sanguine, the hair stuck to her forehead, pillow marks on her bright red cheeks. She wheezed and struggled for breath. She began to laugh hysterically, leaned over him and covered his mouth in wet kisses. After a few minutes she turned over onto her front, and sat up on the bed looking at her phone. He got up, pulled his boxers on, and went to the bathroom to take a piss. Robert wasn't in. He opened the door to the bedroom cautiously and came back in. She lay down on the bed smoking a cigarette, still naked. She looked up as he came in and smiled. As he approached the bed, he noticed the blood smears on the inside of her thighs, and the droplets of various sizes scattered on the pristine white sheets.

'You're bleeding.' He said calmly, despite his horror.

'Oh…I guess I'm early this month.' She replied.

IV

LÈCHE-VITRINE

'Which one?'

'The one over there, behind you, over on your right.'

He shuffled uncomfortably in his chair, and looked briefly over his shoulder. They were sitting in the optimistically designated beer 'garden' of a pub on Dumbarton Road.

'There's a couple of them. Which one?'

'The old one.'

'They're all old.'

'The wan in the, dunno, fucking Panama hat, homburg, or whatever.'

'Homburg or Panama hat? I'm sure there's a big difference between them – inntit?'

'Right, whatever. He's dressed in the beige flannel suit jayket.'

'Ok, I see. That one. What about him?'

'Ma mate Tambo said, right – and he disnae lie about these things…really, he has no reason to make stuff like this up. He has no previous in this respect, and it's no the kinda chat he usually comes up with.'

'Right, well – he told me one time that he played for Motherwell unders and he was on the cusp of being breaking intae the SPL and then…the story broke off.'

'How'd you know he wasn't?' Robert asked.

'Ahve seen him. Seems implausible'

'Aye, granted he's a bit on the rotund side...people get fat, mate...he was in decent shape when he was in his late teens.'

'Canny imagine him looking young to be honest...he's always looked fucking forty.'

'No in school. He looked...aye well he did look a bit older come to think of it.'

'Must have had a tough paper round.'

'Aye.'

'Well?'

'What? Right yeah...so, and I'm sure this is true right – cos, I mean, just look at him.'

The old man in question had piercing blue eyes, long sandy grey hair which drooped down from underneath the sides of his Panama hat. An oxblood paisley cravat tied at his neck, his face had a weathered and pockmarked appearance, and a long thin scar bisected his left cheek. There was a black Labrador asleep at his feet. He continually and methodically turned his glass of Pastis as he spoke; a silver lighter and a small tin of cigarillos lay in front of him. Occasionally he would take one out and twirl it between his fingers before lighting it.

'A sinister looking cunt.'

'Whats yer point?'

'Anyway, aye...so Tambo told me that that old boy over there right, like no joke – he's actually like seen cunts away. Used tae be a mob hitman.'

'Utter pish.'

'Why would Tambo make that up?...He's fae Possil Park as well, his Da knew him growing up.'

'Seems like folklore to me.'

'Honestly man, he's killed hunners a cunts. I believe his preferred method is piano wire. The coppers cannae gie him the jail…he knows too much.'

'Does he still kill people?'

'Nah, don't think so. He's retired. Just sits and bevvies. I suspect it takes a lot out of you.'

'What's with the affectation?'

'It takes a lot out of you, but, you'll have to admit…it must also furnish you with a distinct philosophical tendency, that level of consistent contact with human frailty, violence and mortality… what better education is there? That's probably why he cuts about dressed like von fucking Aschenbach.'

'Nah, I don't buy it. Like, how much does he get paid for each job? Canny be that much – you're likely to be undercut by some cheaper cunt eventually. Especially in this city.'

'It's cheap, right enough – but takes a passion for the job. You're never gonna get rich from it.'

'What's the going rate?'

'Mate, I can have you killed for five hunner quid.'

'Can ye fuck.'

'I'll probably just do it…but I'll wait. Ten years time, you'll be walking around, down Byres Road – doing yer shopping with your stuck up missus, couple a snotty weans running around, and then – boom. Put you out yer misery probably…and you'll remember this exact conversation just as you're bleeding to death. And you'll think…"fuck, he was right."'

'Right, fair enough…how's the teaching going?' He asked.

Robert leaned forward to take a long drink of his pint, apparently to lubricate his vocal chords for the coming exertion…which never came. He sat back in his chair and sighed. He looked Robert over for the first time in a while. The ageing process had left little mark, but he had to admit it was somewhat difficult for him to judge objectively. He remembered holding court on a sofa at an after party, 20 years old, it was after 7am, not a penny of student loan left to his name, dressed in skinny black jeans – a tendrillous mess of back-combed hair sitting atop a half-starved and gaunt head chewing it's face off, the fuzzy carpet turning to mush under his feet, requisitioning the stereo forthrightly, demanding a continuous playing, and interest in, and discussion of, Hüsker Dü's *Zen Arcade* – an album which he had only just bought, but which he was more than willing to demonstrate an intimate knowledge and experience of, not to mention a back-catalog of which he knew nothing…. she, the girl, liquid eyeliner and straightened brown hair, sat across from him half asleep, indifferent, reclining on the floor, making tired eyes at another guy across the room. Frustrated, he got to his feet, stumbled to the kitchen – drinking glass after glass of water at the sink, a throbbing comedown running rampant through the sludge of his brain, trying to stem the tide of inevitable despair and loathing. He turned and leaned against the sink. And then Robert appeared, subdued, a consummate professional, at one with the effects like it was an everyday occurrence, imposing but benevolent, offering a generous hand, warm and clammy to the touch, squeezing his knuckles together painfully as they shook – handing him a whiskey bottle mixed with coke: 'That's a fucking quality album by the way.' And the face remained the same. Tied up in that insolent smile, despite its frame fleshing out – despite the hair growing shorter, and the eyes more grey. Nostos and Algos. Nostos and Algos. Nostos which means something…and Algos which means something else. That's what Carolos, the Greek lad, had said to him once. It serves no purpose. A fault of character, a reflex. Best to dispense with it.

'Anyway…they're trying to pay me off.'

'How?'

'Mostly because I keep kicking up a fuss, I think. I dunno why exactly.'

'Well, maybe it'll help you concentrate on the painting. Or getting a proper teaching job.'

'What d'ya mean proper….like at a fucking Art School? Nah, you're alright.'

'Listen, why the fuck did you do a PhD for if you're no wanting to have a career? Least you won't be skint anymore.'

'I mean I did at some point…suppose I assumed that access tae the intelligentsia was just a formality…a mere matter of obtaining the credentials.' He began laughing manically. 'Yeah...turns out that has fuck all to dae wi it…but whatever it is they need – I don't have it. Probably the right pedigree, let's be honest.'

'Aye, well – least if you got a job there, it'd be full-time.'

'Suppose…but it's a shite state of affairs in any case. I didn't think I'd end up doing this…teaching these kids. They're depressed, man…all of them – trying to get into a uni from an FE college, but it's a stitch up, more rigged than ever…they're alright, most of them. I dunno, I came up in the same way I guess, most of these wee cunts remind me of maself, but they're not…they're not me. They're not bored like I was, they're always agitated, bouncing, half of them canny concentrate on anything. They aren't stupid, they know…they know it's bad. It's a sickness, its systemic, it's an endemic pathology, but they canny learn, they've been conditioned to be obsessed with a lack of something but they can't see what it is, they want enjoyment, pleasure – but they canny attain it. And all of this is reinforced, somehow, societally reinforced – know what I mean? – by everything around them…they have nae chance. I mean…not that I really give a fuck. But they're cannon fodder…

they're just gonna be thrown on the scrapheap. Only gonnae get worse.'

'Well?'

'What?'

'What you gonna do?'

'I guess I'm just gonna pack it in. I can't go through with it anymore. They're gonnae get rid of me anyway.'

'What then?'

'I'll find something. I applied for this one thing. Arts administration.'

'Where is it?'

'Eh?…Aye…erm…aye its down in London.'

'…'

'That boy that did the droney guitar stuff, what's his name, Big Charlie. He's living down there now. He's doing alright. They need someone for their flat.'

'Good stuff.'

'Anyway…what's this party tonight then?'

'It's a dinner party at Clara's studio, with all the other people in the space. It's in the Southside.'

'Right, so what's the script?'

'We'll go and get something to eat, and have a couple of drinks.'

'Nah, I mean wi her. It seems to me that things are progressing, like in a relationship way. I mean, fuck sake…you dinnae have to admit that I predicted this or fuck all.'

'Nah, yer wrong. It's not gonna go the way you think…I'm not exactly sure how it'll pan out.'

'Just be careful mate.'

'How?'

'Because, I've got a feeling about her.'

'Well, you would say that…she's a woman.'

'Right, we're back on that are we?'

'It's unavoidable. What is it then – this feeling?'

'She's just seems like a character from some shite film...but no like one of the films that are blatantly shite, I mean like one that's generally assumed to be reflective of a certain vision, aesthetically pleasing yeah, but on the base of it...it's still shit. It's clichéd, but it looks good. That's probably her favourite film. That's her, she's assumed that mantle, that role – whether willingly or unconsciously. Neither you, nor any other man, had a hand in this – she made herself into it.'

'What film is that then?'

'Right...forget that analogy. She just seems like the type of woman that basically thrives off fucking with you...revels in chaos and drama.'

'It's always good to get some encouragement from yer mates. The fuck you on about anyway? You only saw her once for barely a minute.'

'Yeah...you're right, mate. It's no as if you've been talking ma ear off incessantly about her or fuck all. Listen, I just don't trust her.'

'Because she's a woman.'

'Here we go....alright, fuck it...what if it is then?'

'Well, for start – you're trying to inflict your own damaged perspective onto me...and all because of Laura.'

As he saw Robert's insolent expression markedly drop, he regretted having mentioned this. They were silent for a few moments.

'Fair enough...you're right.' Robert replied. 'But that was a hard won lesson, and I don't regret learning it. The one thing, above all, is that the only time a woman who's crying doesn't seem completely ridiculous is when she's crying over you...cos if she is, then it's a far more serious matter.'

'Fucks that supposed to mean?'

'I'm saying it took me a long time tae extricate myself from that particular influence.'

'You mean from Laura?'

'No her exactly, no...burds in general. They're too embroiled in nature...I don't give a fuck about nature...I don't wanna be reminded of my subordination. I'll take culture every time, even if it only brings the fear. I wanna maintain my vitality, I don't want it to be tainted, compromised...I barely escaped with it.'

'Well...seems pretty fucking specific to me. Seems like your talking about Laura.'

'What I keep saying is...the contexts are different, the circumstances are different, fair enough – but they're all just variations on a recurring theme.'

'You loved her.'

'Dunno...maybe. But what does that signify? Like romantic, emotional love...that's something invented and perpetuated by women...they indulge in it as their form of pornography. I had affection for her...but what I loved was fucking her...I loved the ephemeral pleasure I obtained from her...but after a while, every time after I fucked her, it reminded me too much of dying...and I'm no quite ready to die yet. She didnae care about my work or my ideas, I doubt she really cared about anything...she just wanted me to adapt to own her capricious idea of the good life, to make me into a prop – by making me pitiable, snivelling, supplicant, flabby, and bored...and all out of some petty jealousy. They think we're free and they're jealous of it.'

'Dunno...you're projecting.'

'You can keep telling yourself that, mate. But here listen, think about this…look at the fucking state of you. I mean…you're a fucking mess, mate. Anyone just needs to talk to you for five minutes to realise that – you're wild eyed, rambling…what did I say before? Aye, that's it: a wounded animal. So…burds like her, right, wee chaotic burds…they're compelled to…dunno. Right, yeah. They're compelled to take a certain attitude to you…like they would take towards some wee sickly dog that's had its paws crushed by a car, bandaged up, limping around and whining. That's their thing: wee wounded animals, pathetic creatures which they can nurture and then discard. It's only ever going to be temporary but.'

He got up rapidly, downed the last of his pint and slammed the glass down onto the table.

'Look, there's no need to go off in a huff. Where you going?' Robert asked.

He started to turn on his heel. The old assassin behind them looked up and eyed him shiftily, twirling an unlit cigarillo between his fingers.

'Right, simmer down – I'm just going for a slash. But listen…' He replied.

'What?'

'Don't talk about her like that.'

'Or what?'

'Or we're gonnae have a problem.'

He turned and walked inside the pub. The old man took a small sip of his drink, took his hat off and placed it onto the table, got up, and slowly followed him inside. The black dog woke up instinctively, looked around, yawned, and then lay back down to sleep.

153

...

She sat on a chair wrapped in three jumpers with her legs crossed, stitching a pattern onto a cape…an easel stood at her side, a new canvas begun just two hours before. She looked into the cup and saw the dark liquid move…So, I was just thinking about that time when we were on the beach in Sardinia, and it was awfy cold actually. Mum was a little disappointed, for some reason. She always looks so dour and mournful, and Kath gets that from her… the maudlin sourpuss. It hurts a little and it tingles as well, but it was so good. I would need to get a new appointment, get another prescription. But, in essence, an assimilation of visual language is required – but which language; the language of the objectified body – which body? Mine, of course…the body is graphic, mine in particular…My 'magnificent' body. His skin is so…rough. I should have, though…to be used as a projection somehow, to reflect desire – the banality of it. Some sort of, I dunno…how to phrase it? How to conceptualise it? Auto-erotic autonomism. Oh, that sounds perfect! Maybe look into it, though; sounds too perfect. Maybe it's been said before. Probably. Who gives a shit? He has nice arms. Nice forearms. They're…strong. He should have pulled my hair. There's an issue of the plausibility of solipsism here. Exactly. But where does it end and were does the veracity begin. What attributes should be presented, and recorded – I photograph well, maybe that's the problem? I doubt it. She shivered. The heating wasn't working.

...

'Thanks for coming back. I'm sorry we didn't have time the other day.'

He wasn't exactly ecstatic about it. But needs must. She was incredibly attractive, no more than early forties...brown hair tied up, a few faint wrinkles under her eyes and at the sides of her small mouth. The black shirt open, a silver pendant with a leaf in the middle. They weren't huge, but ample. Weird phrase, ample. Anyway, yes – ample breasts, but the tanned neck was something else – brown with little patches of red, sunspots and freckles. She's been away on holiday. Must be a fairly...you definitely would. He definitely would. Fairly dangerous line of thought given the context. Still, her line of work...must be weird. Maybe it makes it more exciting. Doubt it. She pulled on a pair of rubber gloves, and took his flaccid cock in her hand and felt around. She turned on the machine and picked up the laser, bringing it to the skin. It beeped, it stung like hell – and the smell of burned flesh filled the room. Just an occupational hazard, shagger.

'Ok', she smiled, removing her goggles. 'All gone'.

'Thanks. Is that normal?'

'Oh yes...for a lot people they don't appear at all, but it is a bit unusual for them to appear so quickly, however. Did you inform your partner?'

'Not yet.'

'She'll have to come to get tested too, there are certain strains that are harmful for the cervix and can lead to infertility and potentially cancer. Ok...can I ask you to leave your trousers down for the moment. My colleague will come in, she's a junior resident.'

The junior stepped in, an attractive young blonde with the slightly equine quality that suggested a certain breeding; she had almost certainly played hockey at some point. She smiled nervously at him and snapped on her gloves. She took his cock in her hands and began examining it, for some reason looking up at him occasionally and smiling. The senior doctor continued:

'As you can see, it's best to use Co2 laser vaporisation when a patient presents with one or more hard warts which protrude from the skin. It tends to be preferable to cryotherapy removal – which tends to have an adverse effect on certain types of skin.' The older doctor leaned in and gently stroked the skin of his cock with her gloved index finger. 'As you can see the patient has fairly thin, sensitive skin. This would be at high risk of permanent scarring.'

The junior lifted up his ball sack and felt underneath. Her gloved hands were cold. She took his balls in her hand and rolled them gently. He felt a little stir. 'You definitely know your way around there.' Classic. He should have said that. The junior nodded to her older colleague. They dimmed the lights. With one hand she took a small silver torch – and with the other she lifted his scrotum, shining a brilliant light through it, and running a finger and thumb along its various illuminated red sections. The lights were switched fully back on. 'You can pull your trousers up now.' The older one replied with a worried smile. The junior whispered some words in her colleague's ear. They stepped outside. After a few minutes, the blonde stepped back in and began to speak.

'I just examined you.' She said, looking agitated – and unable to hold eye contact.

'Err, yeah – you did.'

'Now, this is nothing to worry about yet. But, there seems to be something…missing.'

'Really…what exactly?'

'We'll have to do a sonograph. And tests on your semen.'

'What's the matter exactly?'

'It appears, just from the physical exam, that what we call the vas deferens is absent. If this is the case, then I'm afraid you'll find it difficult to father children.' She bowed her head and assumed the appropriate level of deference.

'I see.'

'But please keep in mind that this is just an initial physical examination, there's a strong likelihood we might be wrong – and we'll need further tests to confirm. And if it is the case, then there's so much help on offer nowadays.'

'Ok, but there's no need….I'll take your word for it.' He took his jacket and put it on – unsure of his step, circling and shuffling, a little flustered, a choking sensation at the back of his throat, his voice breaking slightly. He recalled the wet head of his first case of Gonorrhoea. 'You definitely know your way around there.' He said to her as he left.

…

He pulled out his cock and then started pissing. The old boy with the beige jacket from outside came up to the urinal beside him. He looked over, trying to catch his attention.

'You alright, son?'

'Aye, I'm fine.'

'Looks like you had a bit too much laughing gas and no enough Abyss, as they say.'

'Who says that?'

'Some cunt has said it, I'm sure.'

'Right, aye, whatever.'

'You don't seem particularly interested in talking about it… whatever it is.'

'No just now, no. I'm trying tae piss, mate.'

'Who's stopping you? I'm just trying to find the measure of a man such as yerself. I see that you have your suspicions.'

'Listen, mate. I'm no a…'

'A bufty?'

'Not my exact choice of words…but yeah, I'm not.'

'I'll pretend I never heard that…neither am I. You gonnae piss or what?'

'I can't. No if yer yapping away at me.'

The old man turned to face away. He pissed hurriedly, shook the last few drops off and did up his trousers. He heard the old man piss too, a forceful steady stream that lasted almost thirty seconds. They washed their hands side by side. The old man dried his hands quickly and walked out of the bathroom – but as he stepped out a few moments later; there he was again, waiting for him. He rushed up to him and grabbed him by the collar with uncommon force, and pulled him close to his face.

'It seems to me that you have it…it's a curse, or a blessing – a hint of the infernal divine predisposition, as they say. The sacrificial vision.' He let go of him, and smoothed down a slight crease on the arm of his suit jacket.

'Take care, son…Just you take care, now.'

'Aye, whatever.'

…

She lies in bed, the covers pulled up, revealing only her eyes. The sheets are made of satin and are turquoise. She, the other one, the one from before - the eyes are angry, they didn't want to be filmed. The camera lies on top of a silver table outside a bar, on the top right hand corner there is the bridge and a river to the left, it jerks onto a face from below, double chinned – bloated that summer. Two voices. One of them raspy. Persistent, recurring tonsillitis and bronchitis that year. 'If only it were possible to still go east, master the tenets of self-delusion'. A light-hearted discussion on potential suicide methods, and the respective merits and shortcomings of each. A Scene. A wide continuous panning shot of a walk along the *Sentier Littoral* on the *Côte d'Azur* – a spasmodic cut, from behind, the bare shoulders of a brunette with short hair in denim shorts sitting on top of some rocks. She plays guitar badly. Cut to the fountains on the *Promenade du Paillon*. Then to the carnival crowds on the *Promenade des Anglais*. A mouth eating an ice-cream. A view from the top of Ben Vorlich, the summit partially covered in snow. She, another one, from before again, in a bedroom, another one, mouths along to a music video played on a laptop, sang by a girl with peroxide blonde hair. The texture of the synthesisers are bright and tropical. The contralto vocals are unbearably sad. A slow motion snow-storm viewed from a window. She, another one, one for one night only, dark, long, reddish hair at her shoulder – the outline of a magnolia tattooed on her forearm – sitting on the edge of the bed as she ties her shoes, grinning and talking in Spanish on the phone, asking for a cab to pick her up. Pan to the bare room. A fan blows humbly in the corner. No air conditioning. The lens almost fogged from the overbearing heat. Move to the window, the dusky lights of Midtown Mahatten on the horizon. 'So – like, yeah, they totally make you take a tablet – radioactive Iodine. I was radioactive for a day! But no, I'm fine now. The survival rate is 99% or something.' The condolence messages on her page a year later, the screen emanating its pale spectral glow onto the darkened room. A car horn sounds. She gets up and blows a kiss to the camera. The door clicks shut. The camera on a subway, shaking violently, pointed at the floor. Heavy breathing. Bass, a guitar picks out a few notes, clean tone, delayed – a drum machine. 'I just, couldn't, wait, to see you again.' An extended scene: bedroom. Another bedroom. One long continuous shot of the grain of the wall and dark stains. Two people, actors, sitting on the bed. Suitcases lay on the floor. 'Was it hard to come back?' 'I suppose it was. Still feels a little strange.' 'No...I meant with the cases, they're pretty big.' A scene. A friend answers questions in front of a camera. 'I was sitting around the square, drawing – I must have been about fourteen. I was just sketching everything. He had this one drooping eye, walked with his head down – as if the contents of his skull just weighed him downward, bent him forward. He noticed me and came over. Squared up to me. Asked me what I was drawing. I told him to fuck off. He told me to show it to him or he'll punch fuck outta me. I called him a poof, then got out of there quickly. A voice off camera. 'You called him gay...and then ran away?' 'Aye'. A scene. Interior: Boxing Gym, East End. Two Fighters sparring, both young and scrawny. A full crouched counterpuncher and an up-right switch-hitter. They circle. A scene card. White text on a black background. 'Self-Plagiarism'. And then immediately after, another. 'Self-Flagellation'. A monologue, acted out by a reader, sitting, leaning against a crumbling drystone-wall. 'A palliative, infernal, divine/A substitute, some say, for too much wine/Immune to the laws inscribed in Runes/On world Ash Tree spears/And the beginnings of universal pollution/As I sat Beauty down on my lap/She cackled through nicotine stained teeth/And with her consumptive voice/Offered a vulgar joke to those who were gathered there/Her summer scars have faded/ Cauterised by the waters that flow/Polluted, from the fountain of youth/Darkness abounds; no daylight surrounds/And the rivers teem with the blood of the Saints/Now Beauty sits over there/ Running bony fingers through her brittle flaxen hair/The crimson of her painted lips begins to flake and smear/As she discreetly wipes away a single solitary tear/Which briefly graced an overpowdered cheek/Pallid, worn, eroded by too many caresses/And promises, never kept/ Quickly retracted while she noisily slept/ But beauty grows weary of revelry and affected concern/Beauty tires of waiting, stumbles, crawls through the door/A crutch, the reminiscence of some remote night tremor/Which we had hoped behind us...A wilting flower, floating in a sea of detritus.' Back to the camera on the table. 'But he didn't want to die, man...he would have liked to live. He had no choice in the matter'. A scene. And several others like it.

...

The train pulled into the station, and came to a halt with a gentle bump which woke her up. Clara lifted her head up from his shoulder and yawned, rubbing her eyes, opening them wide and then closing them a couple of times. She lifted her phone from the table in front of them, looked at the time and began scrolling through her emails. A muffled voice croaked something over the intercom. She looked out of the window onto the platform, where an intricate latticework of glass and steel curved up from the ground, filling the station with a yellow white glow and then outwards in all directions, forming a cosmic spiral. He got up from his seat and pulled his green rucksack down from the shelf above, and placed it at his feet. He started to lift hers down too, a smaller maroon backpack with brown zips – but it slipped from the shelf, and a misjudgement of its weight on his part momentarily sent it forcefully hurtling towards the ground until he was able to adjust his grip, and guide it down steadily onto the ground. He lifted it up with one hand and shook it inquisitively. She looked around at him and smiled while suppressing another yawn. She got up and stretched her arms. He threw his rucksack over his back and carried hers in his arms. When they alighted at the platform, she turned to him and gave him a peck on the lips.

'What time is the ferry?'

'Oh, we've got plenty of time – stop fussing. C'mon handsome, let's go.'

She started walking forward and reached out her hand behind for him to take. He switched her backpack to his left, clutching it underneath under his arm and took her hand. When they exited the station, she stopped to light a cigarette. He lay her rucksack on the ground. The air was crisp and chilly; the early morning sun shone lightly onto the pale inky sea; a flimsy, near transparent mist teased its half awoken surface and the slumbering depths below. The gleaming white ferry stood rigid, its mechanical drone mingling seamlessly with a multitude of contiguous coastal sounds; the distant but resounding wail of seagulls, and the rustling drip of the frothy ice cold waters of the firth caressing the pebble beach. On the horizon, the islands could be seen – pale green outlines of jagged rocky surfaces and hills, the ethereal pull of their distant shores permitted to function without hindrance across a cloudless sky. She turned to him again and smiled. It was smile which, this time, seemed to lack pretence. She took an over-sized beige cable knit jumper from her rucksack – inside there were three large plastic bottles of mineral water, a make-up bag, a banana and a packet of dry oatcakes. She pulled the jumper over her head, struggling a little to fit through the narrow neck – and then zipped up the old green wax jacket that he'd lent her that morning. They lingered at the edge of the car-park and looked out across the water. She took his hands in her cold fingers and lifted them up to her lips.

'Oh I'm so glad we came, really. It's such a lovely day.'

'I don't think there's anything that I'd rather do.' He replied, looking down at the ground with embarrassment.

He slipped quietly behind, and wrapped his arms around her – resting his chin on top of her head. He sensed her heartbeat quicken, and felt a faint tremor of panic well up, before passing just as quickly. He held his breath.

They walked across the carpark over to the Ferry terminal. She approached the ticket counter with a light skip.

'Good Morning! Can we have two tickets to Brodick please?'

Behind the counter was an old lady with a blonde perm. She looked at Clara severely.

'I'm sorry doll, there's no ferry from Wemyss Bay to Arran. You need to go to Ardrossan.'

Clara turned around slowly, furrowed her brows and screwed up her nose.

'I'm sorry…I was so sure you could get it from here.'

'Did you not check?' He asked, distractedly.

'I was so sure…I remember going before.' She turned back to the counter.

'Where do you go?'

'Rothesay, Bute.'

'Oh, it's so lovely there too.' She turned back around to him.

'Well?'

'Huh?'

'Were you listening?'

'Err yeah, sorry.'

'Do you want to go to Bute?'

'Yes, of course….' He replied, trailing off at the end. 'You know I'll go anywhere with you.'

With a siren's blare the ferry pulled out of the harbour which steadily receded behind them. They walked around from the stern to the bow of the ship, and ascended onto the upper deck where they sat down on the red plastic benches. In front of them and below, a saltire oscillated rapidly in the oncoming breeze – occasionally folding, and then righting itself. The sun too had ascended further, and after 30 unremarkable minutes of cloudy uncertainty, where it presented in timid peaks and slants, it showed itself whole – shining a radiant gleaming light onto the empty deck. Aside from them, there was an old couple, muttering along to a good natured argument through lazy gestures – walking back and forth from port to starboard.

'When did you say your birthday was?' She asked him. She had slipped out of her sturdy brown hiking booths, turned sideways on the seat and lifted her feet, covered in grey woollen socks, up onto his lap.

'The 28th.'

'Oh, that's next week! The big 3-0.'

'Ugh, I don't want to think about it.'

'Hmmm, so what does that make you?'

'It makes me…30, I guess?'

'It makes you…Virgo…born under the Virgin. Makes sense.'

'How?'

'You're a wee bit quiet…and shy.'

'Can't believe I'm turning 30.'

'Oh it's not so bad…come on. I went through it last year.'

'Right, so you're a year older than me.'

'Nine months. Oh I know. Mrs. Robsinson, practically.'

'I'm into it.'

'But, I just found that leading up to it there's just so much anticipation and anxiety, everything is just building up to this moment of something…crisis, or reckoning…but when it happened, I just became completely serene, utterly calm and completely at one with myself – it was like I had somehow come to the other side, and realised how silly it was to be so fraught with worry over it.'

'Why were you worried?'

'The same reasons that you're probably worried.'

'There's gotta be something specific though…'

'I suppose. My older sister Kath…Kathleen. She's a doctor, a gynaecologist or something…she's different, taller, blonde, she got married when she was 28 – she's 32 now. She married this guy… Oh I never liked him, just this boring idiot – he's so stupid. You can tell when you talk to him, there's just nothing going on there…but she was completely in love with him. She was always so brooding… in high school she was kind of cool, I got a lot of music from her – older sisters are good for that. She had this boyfriend, and I liked him – really – he was such a nice person. My parents loved him. He was cool as well…in his way, he had this amazing long brown hair and he played drums. He was always really warm and friendly…oh they were so cute together. I used to hear them singing and playing guitar in her bedroom when I walked past. I'd sometimes stand outside and just listen to their conversations. Anyway, Andrew killed himself the summer before he went to study in Edinburgh. He took some sleeping pills and went swimming in Gare loch.'

'Shit. I'm sorry.'

'I didn't really know a lot about him.' She raised a hand to her face to brush aside a non-existent hair obscuring her eyes.

'Right.'

'Kath was obviously devastated, but she never talked about it. She just got on with her exams, did well and went away to uni. I didn't see her much…occasionally I'd see her out…she was drunk, but it was always quite hard to tell. She'd be home for holidays. We never had a talk about it. Then she met this guy, this whatshisface right…this idiot. Just a smarmy wanker. He wore jeans and shirts tucked in…he played rugby for a while, but then he stopped and he just got this huge belly. He listens to awful music. But if you saw them together, it was so odd. He was sick for a while and it was quite serious. She literally did everything for him. Oh, god I could not do that…be someone's nurse and maid. But she loved him, really.'

Her mouth lingered lazily on the 'L', and she looked up at him with a look of bemusement and surprise. She fell silent and looked towards the approaching land. Some moments passed, until the air between them became thick with curiosity.

'Why did you think about that before your 30th?'

'What?'

'I mean…what made you think about your sister?'

'Oh…yeah, so she's getting divorced.'

'But what…'

'So what about you?'

'Have I ever got divorced?'

'No…I mean, have you ever been in love?'

'That's a difficult question to answer.'

'Why?'

He looked down to the floor, a tiny puddle of water had collected in an indentation on the green surface.

'I guess I have.' He replied.

'Describe it to me.'

'How about you describe yourself first?'

'No chance.' She laughed awkwardly.

'Well, why would I go first if you're not going to?'

'Ok…let me describe you in love, instead.'

'Go for it.'

'You're ebullient, and passionate – but calm and reserved, measured and exacting; when it's there you don't mess around and pretend it's nothing, or try to hide it…And you'll write things to her; little notes, letters, poems, texts – just to try to articulate the intensity, but nothing satiates it…but it inspires you, you never procrastinate, you just work and work and work at it. To perfect it…and yourself.'

'Sounds like a horoscope. Is that how you see me?'

'Maybe that's how she saw it, how they all saw it – the women you were in love with.'

'Maybe. I wouldn't know.'

'Oh I'm sure they were all completely in love with you. I just know it.'

She suddenly became grave, and averted her gaze – removing her feet abruptly from his lap. She stood up and stretched her arms out wide and stood on her tiptoes. She spread her feet apart and brought her outstretched arms down to touch her toes. He watched the denim fabric of her jeans around her arse tighten as she bent over. He started to get a little hard. She turned back around and sat down beside him again, resting a hand on his thigh – drumming her fingers on his kneecap.

'And what about you?'

'What about me?'

'How would I describe you in love?' He asked.

She leaned over and placed her cold hands on his face and kissed him briefly, before turning around to face the approaching harbour. He sighed, and started shaking his leg nervously. He fingered the blue hair bobble on his wrist.

'That's probably a conversation for another time.' She replied, taking his hand and squeezing it.

The glow of the sunlight illuminated the busy harbour, and a throng of people – with suitcases, rucksacks, and shopping bags – standing, laughing, their cheeks rosy from the cooling northern breeze, waiting patiently for the ferry to come ashore.

…

'Yeah.'
'Hello, it's me.'
'Who is it sorry?'
'Don't you recognise my voice?'
'No.'
'It's me.'
'Clara?'
'No…who's Clara?'
'Right…sorry, I was sleeping – just woke up.'
'I was just calling to, I dunno…see how you were.'
'I'm fine.'
'You sure?'
'Well…yeah. I'm alright. What…would it make you feel better to say I'm not?'
'No, don't be daft. I'm glad you're alright.'
'How are you?'
'I'm really good…there's a lot happening here. The people are nicer than I expected.'
'Good stuff.'
'Who's Clara?'
'Some girl, a friend.'
'Doesn't she share a studio with...'
'I dunno. Sorry.'
'Nevermind…ok. Well, I'm glad you're doing ok.'
'Yes.'

…

He and Robert walked down the road in the same direction, but at a safe distance apart, eyeing each other suspiciously – neither seemed prepared to make the first apologetic gesture, though both seemed to want to. Each, in their turn, exhaled in frustration, sighed or muttered incoherently – the air was stale with a mix of regret and impotent rage. Robert went to the counter, placed his bottle of wine on top of it and bought two tickets for the subway. He turned and handed one to him. He took out his wallet, and felt around for some coins in the pouch.

'Nah…you're alright.'

'Cheers.'

They passed through the gate and descended the stairs at Kelvinhall onto the narrow platform, where they were greeted by the distinctive yet vague aroma of burnt diesel fumes and stale air – as well as by a group of five lads standing around at the far end of the platform. Dressed in a variety of women's dresses in several colours, high heels, wigs and embellished make-up – they huddled in a furtive circle, looking around suspiciously. Something was passed around and each partook. The most bewildered of the group, short, pale – skinny hairy legs dangling underneath a bright pink dress that resembled a negligee – seemed to be the focus of discussion and mild ridicule. He laughed awkwardly at the input of his friends. The leader, for there was a leader, had somehow managed to squeeze his plump yet long bovine frame into a sleek black satin dress – and somehow, it suited him incredibly well. In between sarcastic takes and jests, still inaudible, he stood back and ran a thick palm across his thigh – luxuriating in the sensual feel of the fabric and the no doubt odd sensations that it made him experience. His eyes, a pale tired blue, radiated an unmissable kindness and generosity. Robert dropped his lighter to the ground. They all looked up and the down the platform…staring for several moments.

'Ho! It's the fucking Dead Poets Society! Awrite boys! How's it going?' The leader screamed.

'Aye, awrite.' Robert replied – suddenly perking up. He turned back to him briefly and sniggered, before turning back towards the group. 'Where youse off tae then…didnae know Polo was open on a Sunday?'

The leader grinned to his mates – and broke off from the circle. He began walking towards them. The others, hanging back, eventually followed a little distance behind. His hairy fat legs swaying slowly and rhythmically along, he moved at a leisurely yet graceful pace as the thin rap of his stiletto heels clinked a menacing path towards them. His head was bowed, making the bright red curly wig fall slightly from his head – he lifted a hand up to adjust it before reaching his destination, no more than a foot from Robert's face. Robert gulped audibly, gripping the neck of the wine bottle tighter behind his back.

'The fuck you saying?'

Robert started to speak, but his voice merely croaked. He bowed his head and lifted a hand to his mouth to cough and clear his throat.

'I says…where youse off tae…didn't know Polo was open on a Sunday?'

A weighty arm flew around Robert's back, and then around his shoulder, as the platform filled with guffaws and howling laughter. The leader jerked his head underneath his arm, brought it close to his own chest and ruffled the hair on top of his head with his knuckles.

'Nah mate, we're just out on the randan…ma mates getting married…poor cunt, anyway aye…just heading out to the dancing.'

They were incorporated seamlessly amongst the group, exchanging mindless good-natured patter and lewd jokes; some almost had tears in their eyes from laughter as the train arrived and spluttered to a stop. They all climbed inside. The carriage was empty – they sang, they chanted, they laughed more; they beat the sides of the tube carriage gleefully – bouncing up and down on the spot. The train too seemed on the point of bouncing off the track, until it eventually stopped, and they got off – and then two stops later, he and Robert got off at Shields road. They emerged onto the ground level and began to walk. As they walked, the tension evaporated and the conversation started to flow more easily.

'So anyway right...I was watching a video clip on the internet.'
'Never heard of it.'
'Aye, whatever. So yeah...it was this clip from one of those old shows – something like Ibiza Uncovered or some shit, right. Dunno...wanted some retro shit to pop one off to. I was scrolling through and I caught this....'

He took out his phone and played a video, with tinny house music sounds and girls screaming and cheering – the phone lit his face up briefly as they dragged their feet, before coming to a standstill. He tapped once on the screen – beckoned him over, and handed the phone to him. On the screen was a young girl, brown hair with blonde highlights – dressed in a short denim skirt. Her mouth was contorted in an ecstatic and familiar smile, and she was lifting up her white t-shirt to expose her small breasts. Those were familiar too.

'That's her right?'
'Seems like it.'
'She must have been about 18 or something.'
'Yeah...haha...fair enough.'
'You raging?'
'How?'

'No reason…really. But I think if it was me, I'd be a little bothered.'

'Yeah…you would.'

'So it disnae phase you at all?'

'Why would it?'

'Because it seems tae detract from the image which you formed of her.'

'There's no image…no…at least not one that came already formed. There's several images.'

'Well, I guess I have to give you some credit…you do actually believe you're in love with her.'

'I don't just believe it.'

'Whether it's actually true or whether you just believe it…isn't really that important.'

'Are we gonnae have a problem again?'

'No…listen. Let me just say it one more time.'

'Fine, go for it.'

'Love is something desired. Can we agree on that?'

'Not exactly.'

'It's also a form of desire'

'In a manner of speaking.'

'It's more a prolonged and enduring form of desire. It's more consuming, but it's a desire nonetheless. Ok?'

'Here, why the fuck are we getting bogged down in this semantic bullshit? Like, who gives a fuck what it is? Surely, it's function and purpose is its only value?'

'All I'm trying tae say is…fine, maybe you're not exactly like me, right. But this thing wi this burd…there's two separate things here. Cause and object. You're only focusing on the first, because it's impossible for you to know what the true object is. How d'ya no see that?'

'Right, so where does that leave your random occurrences of the sublime in the rubbish heap of desire yeah? Actually, fuck it. I'm no even gonna bother. Yer talking pish. Just fucking leave it. We're here now.'

They stood in front of a weathered and moss covered yellow sandstone building, made in the rotting style once ubiquitous – and surely a tame plagiaristic example even at the time of its construction – but which had, in recent days, become synonymous with some vague perennial classicism which cyclically re-emerges when new ideas are in short supply. It was a former printing house, and as if in remembrance of its erstwhile occupation and function – not practised there for a hundred years or more – the building had grudgingly consented for the pavements immediately outside of its large red wooden doors to be littered with scraps of old newspapers, wrappers, printed notices, and undelivered letters soaked to mush in the unrelenting deluges which inundated this city throughout the year. Robert rolled a cigarette, and stood a little away from the door. He rung the buzzer. A high pitched voice answered, and without waiting for a response – the door buzzed open. They climbed up two flights of stairs and came to a solid steel door which opened with a heavy groan. Behind the door stood Cherie, she looked them up and down, smiled briefly and greeted them. He bowed his head, unable to make eye contact, and felt the blue bobble on his wrist tentatively as his heart rate quickened. She beckoned them inside. Robert nudged gently in front and stepped in before him, a voluble grin across his face.

'Awrite, how's it going? You gonnae charge us entrance then?' he asked, as he began removing his coat.

Inside, a long metal table had been brought to the middle of the vast open space, with makeshift office cubicle walls separating out five different studios areas. Robert approached the table and sat down on one end, nodding in acknowledgment to Clara, who sat at the opposite end talking with a bearded man who he recognised as the manager from the restaurant. Their gesticulations and hand movements suggested concentration, he noticed. The topic of discussion was serious. He could tell that much. Occasionally she would place her hand on his arm and let it linger there before taking it off. She failed to notice his arrival, so he wandered around the different studio spaces until he came to a certain one; her smell lingered in the air, a white coffee cup with smudges of red lipstick on the edges, a book *The Anthropology of Ceremony* which he recalled picking up and scanning that first morning. Difficult to miss her presence. There was an easel standing empty by her chair, and a canvas pinned to the wall above her desk, black and white, curved shapes – branch like connections…he stared at it for several minutes, attempting to decode its effect and was momentarily startled by its sterility. He wandered back to the centre of the studio, and to the table, where the ten people previously scattered around the space had sat down. He removed his jacket and took a seat. She walked over slowly, leaned down and gave him a reserved peck on the cheek – and placed a cold hand on his back and rubbed it slowly up and down as she whispered some small talk. She then returned to her seat at the opposite end of the table, where Cherie had also taken a seat next to her.

    A few bottles of red wine appeared, and a large bowl of salad made of brown lentils, tomatoes, olives and a sort of cheese was brought out and distributed onto plates. People ate slowly, conversing sluggishly about mundane topics to their immediate neighbours. He sat at the end of the table with Robert next to him on his left. To his right was the bald curator from the opening, who asked them hesitant questions in turn, probing for a topic that could prove to have some legs, all the while deciding which attitude to assume. The curator had a curious tick which he hadn't noticed on the previous occasion – when he spoke his eyes would look to one side, and then to the other, as if trying to look behind his shoulder without turning his head. After he drank a couple of glasses the curator seemed a little more at ease, but although his face had grown red and flushed with a certain enthusiasm – there was little doubt as to whether his guard was still up. A couple of people stood up and brought several dishes filled with slices of some form of loaf, with lentils, chickpeas and nuts – baked in the oven so there was a crisp brown covering – and another salad, with mixed leaves, slices of apple, mango and pomegranate covered in a balsamic dressing. He could neither focus on the conversation at hand nor the food, and sat transfixed by the other end of the table where she sat - in deeper and deeper conversation with Cherie. Clara never picked up her eyes or directed her gaze down to the other end of the table, where he was burning a hole through her forehead. Around him, voices and inflections would rise and fall, though predominantly the talk went upwards, snorts of laughter, mutterings – high and low – the sounds of slurping and chewing, and muted and suppressed burping under the breath, the sound of shuffling on chairs, feet tapping on a floor, the rolling click of lighter flames and the soft singe of burning cigarette, followed by a slow exhale. For a moment he saw his mother, younger, smiling to herself, sitting on the bed and chain-smoking her Silk-Cut while watching the TV, a hacking mucus cough occasionally convulsing her serene breathing...then he was back...among all these accumulations of sounds and gestures and movements which fused together, as he sat there, the food uneaten and growing cold on his plate, transfixed on her, on Clara, imagining a conversation which he could not be privy to and the course of which he could only predict with terror. Everything was close, too close around him. He felt a droplet of cold sweat form at the back his neck before falling and gradually making its way down along his spine. The wine further flowed down through the guests, and as they finished eating, one by one they stood up and wandered around the room, changing and swapping places – pulling chairs out from the table – pulling out beanbags and sitting around the floor. He snapped out of that unpleasant reverie and tried to re-engage with those around him. He attempted to pick up the strands of the conversation between Robert and the bald curator that was propelling forward with increasing rapidity. From the other end of the table, Cherie stood up from her seat - re-filled her glass of wine from the table and walked towards him, looking with purpose into his eyes. She pulled an empty chair from the middle and sat it down right beside him. He sat up and stiffened.

'I thought I'd join you guys.' She remarked offhandedly. 'How are you doing?'

'I'm fine, thanks.' He muttered under his breath, unable to make eye contact.

'You hope there's a collapse', Robert continued, 'I doubt there'll be one that's opportune and beneficial…if there's a collapse it'll be comprehensive, apocalyptic, a descent into barbarism and tribalism…it's already happening, actually'

'I think you're being overly cynical.' The bald curator replied, adjusting his glasses and taking a cautious sip of his wine.

'I don't think I am…I miss the optimism of imagining a future as well. But there's nothing except crisis on the horizon.'

'It doesn't have to only be a lament for something lost…it's possible to take concrete actions.' The curator replied.

'You mean gestures…I think. And I suspect they're not that concrete.'

'That's just your cynicism again. It's an easy attitude to take. But something else is required.' Said the curator, perhaps a little too dismissively. Robert sat up in his chair a little and straightened his shoulders.

'Listen…if you're so sure about your so called concrete actions… then how come you're still dressing it up in an obscure lexicon?'

'Eh…certain ideas are complex, and complexity can only be described using a certain language.'

'Listen mate…your ideas aren't that complex. I can understand them and talk about them – but I doubt other people can or want to. If this is the rumblings of some sort of revolutionary moment, then why don't you want other people to understand you? It seems to me that your rhetoric, which you've dressed up in this technological optimism, manifestos and demands – is empty, and designed only to be understood and perpetuated by certain people.'

'On what basis are you saying that? And what makes you think you're representative of ordinary people?' Asked the curator, with a guffaw.

'Well…I'm working class for a start.' Robert replied.

The bald curator leaned back in his chair and looked around the room nervously. He took an awkward sip from his glass.

'How do you even make that classification these days?' He replied. 'It is difficult to judge who is and who isn't part of a working class in the traditional configuration. We're all subject to precarity, instability, and even poverty to some extent.'

'I don't need to make the classification. I may have an education…but I know I still am. You're trying to deflect…seems like you don't want to talk about it honestly.'

Although no voices had been raised, he felt the attention of the room being perceptibly directed towards the end of the table where he was sitting. He looked down towards Clara, who smiled and nodded her head – mouthing something which he couldn't make out. She got up and came over, taking a seat next to the curator and opposite Robert. Cherie cleared her throat and began speaking.

'I don't think that's the case...Nathan always talks about intersectionality in his writing; and that includes class, and race, and sexuality and gender.' She added, looking askance towards Robert.

'I wasn't talking about those other things...I was talking about class.' He replied.

'Why should we only talk about class?' She asked him. 'There are complex structures of power relations at play and systems of oppression that intersect with each other.'

'Well...because I doubt any of them intersect anywhere near you, doll.' He replied curtly.

Cherie's face grew flushed with anger. 'What the fuck is that supposed to mean?' She asked, almost through gritted teeth.

'Sorry...seems like I've broken some sort of etiquette here by bringing up class?'

He felt, at this point, the need to interject...and immediately wondered why he had not already done so. He knew why...he was paralysed by some jealousy, fear, and then confusion – but now things seemed to be evolving in ways which...He stood up and took the half-filled bottle of red wine and topped up everyone's glass before sitting back down, and slowly clearing his throat. It seemed to alleviate some of the tension, but in addition created an expectation on him to contribute – which he didn't really feel like doing.

'I think the issue he's trying to get at,' he began prudently 'is that there's an absence of discussion of class politics now...it seems to be tacked onto a multitude of things which are maybe related in some contexts, but also detract from a discussion of the issue on its own – which still needs to be addressed.'

'Purposefully distract…I would say. There's no need to be diplomatic here, mate.' Robert replied, gravely.

'So what did you mean before? And I don't appreciate being called doll.' Cherie asked, her cheeks still tinged red.

'Oh fuck off…I wasn't even meaning you specifically - it's no only about you all the time…Doll. What I mean is...'

'Mate..' he tried to say. But it was already too late.

'This fucking polite bourgeois subjectivity all of youse have insulated yourselves with…just so you don't have to deal with cunts like me on a daily basis…I might have read a lot and look and sound different, but I've been here the whole time…but you can only believe in the existence of a working class if its impotent, degraded and ignorant…I'm not authentic enough for you.'

'Mate…'

'No…it's all just moralising without a purpose…bereft of any substance or genuine sentiment…you're guilty about something, but not really guilty enough. At least I'm not disingenuous about my guilt…I'm guilty as fuck. At least I can come out and say it. Youse, on the other hand, throw about some bullshit word –and then feel like that's explanation enough.'

At this, Cherie became suddenly animated – jabbing a finger accusingly at Robert, a few inches from his chest.

'I'm sorry, but that is just unacceptable. Your original words and expressions are needlessly violent…you're using toxic language to over-power and demean, just because you don't like what I'm saying. That is not ok.'

'Sorry…I was under the impression we're striving towards equality?'

'Why the fuck is that relevant?'

'Well...do you want complete equality or do you want special pleading? Because if it's complete equality...that includes being a victim of...violent language at any rate.'

'Mate...'

'It doesn't have to be like that...we can and should adjust the discourse, and the terms and modes of expression so they're more accommodating.' She replied.

'Yeah...ok. Let's be more accommodating...let's imagine everything is conducted in a language which suits everybody's ever-evolving sensitivities...still doesn't change the fact you have fuck all to say.'

'Right...this is getting tiresome now. I think you just need to be aware of your position and the power that it entails...it's not just about class.' Cherie said, with the condescending finality of a schoolmistress reprimanding a wayward but harmless child.

'Oh shit, yeah...maybe you're right? Actually, no...you're dead fucking wrong. I'm aware and I'm contrite as far as it goes...but I don't have my hands anywhere near the levers of power, economic or cultural – nae cunt like me ever has. But at least I try to see beyond...to a point where people don't only seek to be defined by identities which are set by the dominant ideological power... that's all you're doing...maintaining and sustaining categories for people. At least I think that like, although I'm no exactly the same as someone, I can still try to understand them and their experience on some level...but I don't think you're capable of that. All you really care about is how people talk. Being hysterically aggrieved isn't radical...doll.'

'Hysterical?' Cherie leaned back in her chair, drank from her glass and looked at Clara. 'Thanks for explaining that to us. We really appreciate it.'

After a minute or two of awkward silence, the conversation had moved on without much effort. He'd already drank too much wine, and began to feel unsteady on his feet. He wandered around the space and came across an old brown couch on the corner next to a fire exit; its upholstery was peeling off at the arms, and it smelled of stale cigarette smoke and turpentine. He sat back and started picking at his fingernails, biting at them and peeling them off at the edges. He looked up and saw her making a line towards him, the fingers of her right hand gripped around the stem of a wineglass – the other hanging uneasily at her side over a small black handbag, the yellow white of her hair mute in the dim light – her face still without expression. Cherie came and sat down beside him. She pulled a pack of cigarettes from her handbag and offered him one, which he refused. He felt his body tense up.

'You feeling alright?' She asked, while lighting her cigarette with a pink bic lighter.

'Yeah cool, I'm just a wee bit tipsy.' He replied.

'So about the other night.' She began 'It seems to me that you're having a bit of trouble connecting...like there seems to be something blocking you. I can help you with that.'

'Err...right. I dunno what you mean.'

'I practise bodywork...and I can work with you, physically and emotionally, to try and unblock whatever issue it is you have.'

'What issue?'

'Your issue with intimacy. I can provide a safe environment, I have a lot of spare capacity at the moment to deal with other people's mental health issues, and I'm trauma literate. And my nesting partner Nathan, has said it's ok to bring clients into our home space.'

'I don't think I really understand what's being offered here... are you trying to sell me something?'

'I work pro-bono.'

'Sorry…I mean, you seem great, really, but I'm seeing someone. But, really…it's nothing to do with you at all. You seem lovely.'

'I wasn't…you don't really understand. I'm offering you a professional service.'

'Right…right, well I'm afraid I have to decline…sorry.'

'Fine. I was also going to tell you. I found out I have genital warts; so you should probably get tested.'

'I see…yeah I guess I'll go and do that.' He got up to his feet abruptly.

'Just going to the toilet.' He muttered absentmindedly.

She looked at him, unfazed, and her lips briefly curled into a caustic expression

'Well…you should check to see if you have any warts on your penis.' She replied.

He walked back over to the others, who were milling around near the table, and hovered among them. Clara was nowhere to be found. He thought that she might have left and became stricken with a momentary hollow feeling in his gut. Nathan, the bald curator, was smoking weed from an electronic vaporiser and discussing the mechanics of a universal basic income; Robert sat in front of him – but did not appear to be listening. He rushed over to Clara's studio space, but she wasn't to be found there. He focused on the branch painting hanging above the desk – lingering over it for a few minutes. A throat was cleared behind him, and then a voice spoke.

'Oh…what are you doing in here?' She asked. He turned to face Clara who was peeking her head over the edge of the partition.

'Looking at your work…'

'This isn't me…I'm over there.' She reached in and grabbed his hand and pulled it towards her. She led him into a studio on the opposite corner and sat down on the only chair. The walls were bare – and on the small wooden desk there were some blue ballpoint pens in a silver and red tin, and next to it a notepad. In the corner there was a small plastic kettle and a jar of coffee. She boiled some water and made herself a cup. She opened the notebook and started scribbling something.

'Your mate…' she began without looking up '…he's a bit of a dick, right?'

'He is…' he replied, 'but he's alright.'

…

The door to his bedroom was slightly ajar. He hadn't gone in to work at the archive that day and, like the day before, had called in sick. The bedroom was cold and it was raining outside. He was lying in bed and it was late in the morning. The order which he had forcefully imposed on his surroundings had, in fits and bursts, eventually come undone – the flat had grown uncomfortable with its new tame state and agitated; clothes and socks burst out from the drawers and spread themselves across the floor, scraps of paper appeared and then multiplied until they covered all the surfaces; on the bedside tables there were numerous plates of uneaten food, mugs of cold tea, several ashtrays full to the brim, and cans of lemonade so filled with soggy fag-ends they spilled from the tops. Yesterday he had waited until 4pm to leave the house, impelled by nothing other than a nagging need to do so. He managed one turn around the street, and finding himself short of breath and panicking – he sprinted back to his room and shut the door. He was a fellow a little before thirty, above average height, and of a pleasant exterior occluded by unpleasant thoughts; in his dark eyes there were an overabundance of ideas, and a surplus of concentration given to each. He was lying in bed and it would soon be the afternoon. It is difficult to envision how it may occur, and when it does, it's easy to miss the all too subtle signs. It is impossible to imagine how the mind, and the thoughts which sustain it, can at once turn completely against yourself. At first there is a minor thought which swells until it is ready to burst forth from the cranium – then backs down, nullified by logic, temporarily at least, and then it returns, again, but this time it lingers, it connects with others – and then more, and more still, and eventually they form a constellation of swirling sentiments that become indistinguishable from one another – they mutate to ailments, and maladies and illnesses; they jostle for attention with urgency, they become corporeal, the brow sweats, the throat dries, the pulse races. He ran his fingers over the blue bobble around his wrist and pulled it out further than it had ever gone before, but as he closed his eyes and prepared for the inevitable sharp pain, he felt it snap. He opened his eyes and looked at the frayed blue band between his fingers. He began coughing and breathing heavily. The hand in which he was holding the blue band began to shake violently. He was lying in bed, and it was yesterday morning. There was a knock on the door, and Robert entered without waiting for an answer, pulled a seat from the under the desk and sat down facing him.

'Listen…aye, so…I got that job in London.'

'Oh aye…Good stuff.'

'We'll see…I'm gonna go down tomorrow for three weeks and meet with Big Charlie and check out his flat.'

'Right…so you're going away?'

'Aye.'

'No worries.'

'Eveything cool?'

'Sound, aye.'

'Here's a wee something for you...I don't like it.' He unrolled a white canvas with a dark blue painted circle obscured by a thin covering of white and showed it to him briefly, leaving it on the desk.

'Cheers.'

'Well...Keep that head up, chief.'

He jumped out of bed, quickly washed his face and pulled on some clothes – a t-shirt, a red jumper, and an overcoat – before hurrying out of the flat. As he made his way out onto the street, he was unable to see more than a foot in front of his step; everything else in his field of vision became hazy and distorted. Although it was now sunny, with sharp cold gusts of wind, he was covered in a clammy sweat underneath his clothes and shivered uncontrollably. He ran along the street, and across roads, barely missing the traffic, oblivious to the blaze of car horns he was leaving in his wake, until, out of breath, his limbs and muscles burning from fatigue, he came to a stop. A bus approached and he got on...he managed with difficulty to take his wallet from his pocket but couldn't stop his hand from shaking enough to rummage through the coin pouch. The driver became annoyed and drove the bus forward – he swayed back and forth, still trying to find the change, until the bus reached the next stop where it came to a sudden halt. He fell forward and cracked his head on the thick plastic partition. The driver began to shout. He got up and crawled through the door until he was outside again. Everything had now become a blur of whitish light in his eyes and the manifold sounds of his surroundings. Someone approached and asked a question. He shook his head. He started to run again, at full speed this time, until his legs grew tired – and then he would jog, before running again; somehow the lining of his coat had become torn – he stopped and pulled his arms out of it and threw it onto the floor before continuing to run. He ran over a footbridge across the river, and down desolate streets of shuttered industrial buildings and down long winding labyrinthine roads until he collapsed in the middle of an empty leafy street. A pedestrian prodded his pitiful carcass with its foot as it passed him by. He awoke, dazed and startled – the sun was beginning to set. He got to his feet and walked the last few hundred metres to his destination. The panic began to take hold again as he reached her door. He lifted up his fist and punched himself in the face twice, full force, and rang the buzzer. A soft melodic yet puzzled voice spoke. 'It's me.' He called out. The door opened and he walked into the close and made his way up to the third floor. Standing at the door was an elegant woman in her mid-fifties with dark brown hair, specked with grey, tied into a neat bun. She wore a long knitted grey skirt, a buttoned up white silk blouse with a beige cardigan over her shoulders; around her neck was an elaborate necklace of silver and emerald green stones. Her brown eyes were heavily made up, but there was a moist redness to them that betrayed the recent presence of tears.

'Can I help you?' She asked.

'I'm here to see Clara.' He replied loudly, struggling to adjust his volume.

'Oh, of course…come in. I'm Clara's mother. She's just changing her contact lenses in the bathroom.'

He introduced himself bashfully. All at once, he felt her questioning and accusatory gaze over him as she guided him down the hall, and towards the couch in the living room, avoiding a direct appraisal of his doubtlessly wild appearance. Moments later, Clara came back from the bathroom – her eyes red and swollen. She jumped when she caught sight of him. She sat down on the edge of the armchair. The mother got up and went through to the kitchen. The gradual sound of a kettle boiling could be heard.

Clara sat down on the armchair and scowled at him through her moist red eyes.

'Is everything ok?' She asked.

'Err yeah...I fell over in the street there.'

'It's awfully cold...didn't you bring a jacket?' The mother asked, as she re-emerged holding a tray with a teapot and three cups.

'Err...no...I must have misjudged the weather.'

'And what happened to your face?' The mother asked.

'He fell over...' Clara interjected.

'Yeah...I fell over...in the street...I tripped.'

'Oh dear, maybe you should go to the hospital...you might have a concussion.' The mother said matter-of-factly, and without great conviction.

'No, No, I'm fine...it's stupid really. I tripped...tripped on the curb. Nothing hurt but my pride.'

'We didn't know you were expecting a guest, Clara.'

'I must have forgotten that you were coming.' Clara replied. She looked up briefly and gave him an irritated look.

'Well, of course it's fine...I'm just awfully sorry we don't have anything in to offer you; she's not very good at remembering to do the shopping, or anything. When did we buy this place? I'm sure I've forgotten now. I remember it took an awfully long time for you to arrange the decorators and to have the kitchen done.'

'Oh it wasn't that long...come on.' Clara replied.

The front door was closed with a bang, and a voice called out. 'I got a bloody ticket!' A man with a full head of thin dark grey hair walked into the living room, a jovial smile fixed onto a ruddy wrinkled face; he wore a white shirt with a checked pattern and an olive coloured moleskin jacket. The father immediately approached him and shook his hand vigorously.

'So, you must be the boyfriend...we've heard a lot about you!'

'Dad.'

'Oh hud yer wheest...I'm only having a wee jape. All good things, I assure you. Now, what are your intentions with my daughter?'

'Dad...'

'Oh come now Clara, he knows I'm only joking.'

'I was in the area and I just thought I'd pop by...'

'And I see you've injured yourself there...been in a fight have we? Hate to see what the other guy looks like!'

'No, no, no...I fell over. I tripped on the...curb and fell over it.'

'Ok...let's have a wee look at you then, shall we.' The father approached and took his head and tilted it from side to side. They locked eyes, and for a moment he was able to distinguish a certain potential, behind the cheerful exterior of those pale blue pupils.

'Hhmmm, yes – there's a fairly prominent contusion under the eye and some swelling...but no cuts. Ach, you'll live...just have yourself a wee dram and you'll be back in tip top condition. Do we have something in the house Margaret?'

'You're on call darling!' The mother replied.

'Oh damn, yes...she's right – but so needlessly dramatic. Theatrical personality...she dabbled in acting as well, you know – in her youth. Hard to believe now, I know. She used to vote Conservative and now votes Green. Odd transition. So, you'll have had your tea?'

'Actually', Clara began, 'We were going to go out for dinner... that's why he came around. Sorry, I forgot we made plans.' The father's face became suddenly grim, and his garrulous demeanour seemed to evaporate instantly. He crumpled his brow and looked ominously towards his wife.

'Ah ok...so I suppose we should get out of your hair. No point us old folks hanging around and cramping your style.' He walked over to where the mother was sitting and stood hovering over her – and then reached down and placed his arms on her shoulders pulling her upwards firmly to her feet, and then ushered her over towards the door.

'Goodbye darling…we'll call you. I think your mother isn't feeling well anyway…I should really get her home.' The front door closed.

Clara got to her feet and started silently pacing up and down the room, looking up at him and back down to the floor. He began to feel dizzy.

'So what's wrong with you?'

'I tripped…'

'No…you didn't.'

'I ran here…I wanted to see you so badly…I tripped.'

'Well…I was busy. You're looking a bit thin...have you been eating?'

'It's broken.'

'What is?' She asked.

He held up his wrist pathetically.

'Oh…well, hold on.' She walked quickly out of the living room. Rosie came in just as her owner was leaving and stood at the doorway, yawned extravagantly, and identified the intruder on the couch. She made her way over to assess the situation, approached his outstretched leg and coiled her fluffy body underneath and around several times. She then stood still and looked up towards him. He reached his trembling hand down to caress the fluff on top of her head and she started to purr – but the sound of the door slamming startled her, and she lunged forward and dug her sharp front teeth into the skin of his middle finger. Clara came back in. She stood over him and threw five yellow pills in a blister pack onto his lap.

'Klonopin. That should tide you over. And I've called you a taxi: it's on the way.'

...

At first there was a mere urge, and then...Three days in, four before his birthday, the same bed and similar clothes – similar but not the same; then of course there were the sorties, or attempted excursions to acquire food...he'd reach the street outside, or a little beyond, but it swarmed all around him far too quickly, debilitating him. And it had started routinely enough, but after the first, then the second, and then the third curt response, from four, to three, to one word...to nothing. There were no more responses, so now he was here. He hadn't been to work in...lying in bed looking at the ceiling and then out the window for hours or longer, and then longer – from when the yellows of the streetlights dimmed to accommodate the coming dawn to when they would awaken again in the hazy darkness, he'd lie mostly still – sometimes turning on his side...looking at his phone – but there was nothing. He'd fall asleep and then wake up, euphoric almost...taking occasional sips from a bottle of water....and on the third day, a resolve, to attain some form of final judgement at least...but message, after message accumulated on the screen in countless unanswered lines...sent forth into that electric void, where no one was listening...and then there were no more messages, at least ones which he sent through his phone...they were composed in thoughts instead, written into the ether and remaining there, paralysed. At first there was a mere urge, and then...determination...but even then there was indecision, despite it being a singular obsession throughout the course of his no longer young life...the final ignoble act of defiance, made out of spite if nothing else – at first the scenarios were dramatic and revelled in baroque spectacle, and then became less so...yet, the merits of each were weighed against the means; a cowardly desire to avoid pain permeated...the fourth day was composed of two sights; the first, a pigeon skulking on the window sill and tapping its beak onto the glass before flying off...the third, or rather the second...yes the second...the second was the plate... glimpsed through dry burning eyes...a plate with a half-eaten ham sandwich, mossy green on the crust, beginning to rot after three days, no...more...he picked up the plate and with what little strength he could muster - smashed it against the wall, and felt all at once liberated from a certain tyranny – and what's more he had discovered the conceptual solution...a grain of rice and a sesame seed. It was his flesh. The flesh was weak, without a doubt. Best to get rid of it. Within the district of Kotthivala, in the village of Khandakavitthika, lived the chieftain of the clan named Samgha – who had seven sons. It was to him that King Tissa sent a messenger demanding that the strongest one of them be called up to serve as one of his select warriors. The seventh and youngest son, Sura, had the strength of 20 elephants but was looked upon with suspicion by his older siblings – due to his propensity for idleness and dissipation. Around the village, they called him 'spirituous liquor' – owing to his unrivalled drinking prowess. His brothers were pleased that he was to be chosen to serve the King; yet his parents were distraught, as they were fond of their youngest child, who was mischievous, kind hearted and seemed to infuse the house with good-natured levity. The King called upon Sura – who was brought forewith to the palace, and entrusted with an important task. He was to watch over the sacred Bodhi Tree, which had travelled across many seas and rivers, grown from the right branch of the very tree under which the exalted Gautama had reached enlightenment...in the middle of the fourth night there were cramps which grabbed at his innards, twisted at them, and tied them in knots. His skin cracked and blistered. If only he could go and buy some rice and sesame seeds…Ah mean, only need the wan of each a go, really…but on the fourth day…no the fifth day…the fifth day he spent in bed, obviously…unable to move his body, which he could feel withering and shutting down…and then the next, probably, and the next, and others – only his eyes would work, they stayed open and would then close…he couldn't control them. 'I should have been honest with you…it was pointless to pretend I hadn't succumbed from the first moment I saw you. But I don't think this would have made a difference' And then, and then…eventually he didn't wake up at all; there was no pain, and suddenly everything in the world became light. The feeling of the mattress underneath his body lessened, and he could feel it coming up, at first cautiously, a millimetre up – then back again, halfway down – then further up, then up again (by a centimetre, this time) and then by an inch…and further up, and up towards the ceiling, until twenty minutes later…some time later… some time – Time, which probably didn't really figure within this context…he was at the ceiling, floating two meters above his bed, weightless, cushioned and supported by waves of air. He turned over to face down towards his bed…but there was no trace of his human body. No sense in looking for a shop-worn cliché on the other side…he was sure that he'd attained it nonetheless. All that was once lived has receded into…He was gripped by hysterical laughter, which made no noise at all. He wasn't transparent and seemed to be wearing the same black jeans and grey t-shirt he had decided – out of laziness more than anything – that he would die in. He moved around the air like one would swim…and then discovered that thrusting your body forward, with your arms pointed and together in front, would increase the speed, which became faster and faster, and the only way to stop was to go from a horizontal position to a vertical one, standing up in the air. He discovered this, as usual, the hard way – as he careened forward overzealously and hit the window. It didn't hurt. Afterwards he floated down to the floor and, placing at first a hesitant foot on the ground, and then another – found that that he could stand, and walk. He walked around the flat. It was a fucking mess. He became concerned and a little pissed off because...the way it would work was that, right, yer definitely allowed to fly around as much as ye want, right – but see if you put your feet down oan the flair...its over mate – nae mare flying for you. Turns out that was bullshit – cos he jumped back up and, sure enough, he was back floating around, going mental – bouncing aff the walls. He put some banging tunes on and bounced around some more. 'I'm not going to pretend that I'm not in love with you...and you must know that I am, even though it's only been a few weeks. But I know absolutely nothing about you. I know nothing because you've given me nothing to go on...no clue, no hint...no.' He actually tired himself out...mostly because he was trying, unsuccessfully as it happens, to jumps through the walls. Didn't work. Bullshit. So he tired himself out, like actually, and had to go and have a wee lie down. Got bored of that fairly soon...opened the windaes and just fucking went for it...pure floating around outside like some mad radge... nae cunt was around...he floated down to the pavement, on terra firma, as it were....took a wee walk to the shops tae buy some baccy and, dunno, a bottle of ginger or summit...or ice poles...bit cold for that...thing is, right, and I'm no talking pish...nae cunt could see me...I was invisible...pure flapped my arms in front of the shopkeeper but he never batted an eyelid...then I grabbed him by the nose and gave it a wee squeeze...never even felt it...gave him a slap right in the puss, justae make sure – and right enough, nothing untoward happened. Grabbed a few packs from behind the counter and bolted...didn't really need tae...nae cunt was following me. Ah jumped up intae the air again...and began to floating around at a whim, in a state of reckless euphoria – uncaring and exhilarated, flying close to the windows high above, and observing the people in their windows going about their everyday tasks; mostly lying down on couches, their faces illuminated by blue screen light, in beds, half-clothed, some naked, cooking, cleaning, eating, masturbating... fucking, shitting, pissing and showering. He would open up the windaes and throw things at them; scraps of paper and wrappers from his pockets, bits of chewing gum, cigarettes...pure belting them right aff their heids...no response. 'My son, I've taken this opportunity to write – I see no other way to express the complexity of feeling instilled in me by your absence, or rather, lack of existence...My son, it doesn't really work if you're not a son...this letter to my non-existent progeny...it wouldn't work if you were not similarly cursed. The only advice I can give you is this...always jump in...always believe in your own mythology...never abandon the work...and stay away from fireships.' He soared up to the skies and cut a path through some thick grey clouds, bursting them in his stride, before climbing higher above them, and looking downward; the muddy white of the river snaked across the city, which, from such a great height, seemed to be completely empty. He tried to rise further but it was impossible...a strong force seemed to keep his ascension in check, locked in the stratosphere with no possibility to rise higher. There was a limit - the limit was apotheosis...he knew that much...so he climbed back down gradually until he was in line with the rooftops – and then floated East along the river and then up towards the Green, where he descended into the midst of a crowd gathered there. They seemed to be waiting for him, dressed in black and grey petticoats, tweeds and cloaks and chesterfields – gripping canes and umbrellas, bowler hats removed from their head and held to the chest – a wooden stage had been erected...he landed onto this stage, the crowd bowed their head in solemn deference...some men approached and placed on him the white smock of the condemned and bound his hands in rope; unable to make eye contact – they too bowed their heads and simply offered the black mask for him to place over his own head...and with outspread hands they presented to him the empty noose...he climbed onto the block, then thought...fuck it...took the daft white smock and black mask aff his heid and floated away uptae the skies again. They were pure raging. 'There was, I believe, something behind that voice, which spoke a simple but recondite language...a thunderous wail cloaked beneath that soft soothing tone...but I couldn't quite grasp its meaning.' He floated on his back among the clouds and fell into a reverie...many of them were gathered around the café table, sheets of paper and notepads spread out among them; plates of half eaten *andouille* and *tartare de boeuf*, seeping brown and dark red juices – he looked at these with revulsion... thick clouds of smoke clogged the air...he sat to the left of a small man with beady eyes in round glasses and short black hair, the fringe cut clumsily in a jagged straight line...he spoke, and smoked, and occasionally coughed; they all listened – he spoke softly, but his words were vital and carried great import for those around him. And then they turned tae me, and ah cleared ma throat and ah says...'You see right...the Catholicism came from my mother... who upheld its patriarchal lessons with matriarchal diligence...see what ah did there?' but they were having none of it...I told them tae get tae fuck and bolted. He floated down onto the street and went into the nearest pub. Inside the publican stood behind the bar, conversing with his regulars with his huge beefy arms, covered in greenish blue ink, resting on the counter; his face smeared in a solid block of black stubble tinted with hints of grey, his barrel chest larger yet more hollow, the pale serpent eyes now grown weary and wise with hard won experience, the veins at the temples now static. He laughed and joked and reminisced good-naturedly about the past; broken, domesticated and civilised. 'What I lack is the appropriate form…I have no means to convey this to you; there are no forms left which can carry the authenticity of this message, which after all is modest – but demands to be rarefied, to be worshipped and made glorious…there are no forms which haven't been made trite by the clumsy intervention of a billion unsteady hands. I have no new form to give…but neither do you have anything to give in return, really.' He left the pub and trudged along the street…it was a Saturday Night…packs of crowd prowled the street spilling into bars, piling in and out of taxis, collapsing on the floors, shoving, swearing, laughing…the pavements strewn with litter and vomit, and chips and cheese. He walked amongst it all – not having the heart to float at a safe distance above. Despite being dead he felt the cold. It was unforgiving and made no distinctions. It was, in balance, a neuro-philosophical proposition…but certainly more philosophy than neurology. When he had been alive, there were only a handful of instances where he could perceive the truth…or a claim to truth at any rate…it was a truth presented without equivocation or confection, devoid of gloss or made palatable by being shrouded in the panacea of beauty…he recoiled from them, even now as memories…but held them close nonetheless. It was, in retrospect, those brushes with truth that kept him isolated and frozen from the vitality that still surrounded him…the life-force…that also endowed him with a certain disposition…once a luxury…now ubiquitous and thoroughly democratic…he never doubted for a second that this ontology was the way of all young men; some, however, had the strength to manage it. It was a disposition that makes you hollow, there is nothing but the interior – but the inside itself is empty; and in such a state, the performance of any action cannot occur without the feeling that the action itself is without purpose...and then one begins to despise the injunction to perform, and the various illusions that sustain it. It is a seductive certainty...this ancient truth; it echoed endlessly through the ages, as the brutal simplicity of the old world disintegrated and the cold contours of the new began to solidify around it and then, just as quickly, melted into liquid, before evaporating in bursts of static. It is a comforting fatalism... and the numerous prescriptions he had dutifully consumed could only obviate and keep it temporarily at bay...there is no chemical solution to a philosophical problem. Even in death, amongst the crowd. He walked up and down for hours...the crowds thinned out and then eventually disappeared. He stood alone. But no...this can't be it...this amusing yet banal purgatory...nothing more than a *petit mort* – a precursor to the actual, second and more final. And just like that he rose up and found himself floating down towards river, and across the squinty bridge, heading south...headlong into the abyss.

He came upon the blonde sandstone tenement on that leafy and now familiar street as if returning to the scene of a crime, and paused at the door in front of the buzzer, reaching for it instinctively before stopping himself. He left his feet and floated hesitantly above the ground, gradually moving upwards until he reached the third floor. The curtains were open, and he observed the creases of duvet over a compact lump underneath, which stirred and changed position. A grey dawn was beginning to break. He pulled the stiff window upwards, the wood, wet with early morning dew, made a squeaking sound...the lump under the covers moved suddenly in response...he froze...waited...and after a few moments he floated into the room. It was still dark...the warmth within was stifling...

he got down onto his feet and tiptoed around…and pulling a chair from the desk, he placed it to the left hand side of the bed and sat down. She flipped onto her side facing him, and the covers slipped down, uncovering her face and naked breasts…he looked away immediately, out of the window – and listened to guttural rumblings of a rubbish truck somewhere off in the distance. After a few minutes he had summoned enough courage to return his gaze to her. She opened her eyes…and then closed them again, drifting off to sleep. He watched her; the gentle rise and fall of her chest, the light squeak of her breath as the air evacuated her lungs – but for now he steered clear of the face…occasionally the rhythmical breathing was interrupted by utterances, noises and vocalised fragments which struggled for meaning. After a few hours he had settled into this meditative contemplation, but at 9am – the silence was broken by the shrill tone of an alarm playing on the phone at her bedside table. She opened her eyes, and without looking, reached over and tapped on the screen with her right index finger. She suddenly sat upright on the bed and threw the covers off. She rubbed her eyes with the knuckles of both hands and yawned. She stared directly past him, out of the window, longingly…she blinked. He got up from his chair. She stood up and made the bed, then brushed passed him and walked towards the door. Her scent lingered in his nostrils. He followed her down the long dark corridor. Rosie came in from the kitchen, stopped short and looked up at him with a puzzled expression, then yawned and made her way into the bedroom. He went to the door of the bathroom and could hear the rapidly beating sound of water, he edged the door open but all at once felt a stabbing shame…he lingered at the doorway as clouds of hot damp steam pummelled his face. He heard coughing and retching…and then a few minutes later the sound of a sharp and steady electric vibration and her suppressed orgasmic moans. She came out of the bathroom, flushed red on her cheeks, and pushed past him, dressed in a yellow bathrobe with a white towel monument covering her hair. He followed her back into the bedroom. She took off the bathrobe and stood naked by the side of the bed, the drone of the hair drier blowing her hair over her eyes. She picked up a brush and crunched it through her hair. She walked over to the drawers and pulled on a pair of plain black pants, and then went back over to the desk and sat down on the chair. She looked into the mirror…and he looked at her reflection. She started to screw up her face, going through a succession of expressions of surprise, hurt, joy and elation. She took a long thin cigarette from the pack on the table and lit it with a match. She took a few drags and left it at an angle on the clear glass ashtray. She looked into the mirror again, took a black cylinder from the drawer and started applying the red lipstick. She got up and walked over to the clothes rail and pulled out a dark blue cotton dress which she climbed into, one foot at a time…he walked over to her and stood behind her as she struggled with the zip on the back…he glimpsed the downy transparent white hair on her shoulder and reached out a hand to touch it, but it merely hovered an inch away – unable to make contact. She came to the bed and lay down on top of the covers, picking up a glossy magazine from the bedside table and flicking through it inattentively. He walked over to the other side of the bed and lay down. He looked to the left, and found a crisp new paperback which hadn't yet been read. He opened it up and creased down the card of the front cover and skipped the preamble, turning to the first page. He cleared his throat and began to read out loud, in a clear and confident voice:

'The desiring subject only acts with experience and this experience is opaque but nonetheless emanates from him/her – the subject's experiences is governed by that of another, who confronts them with the fact that the subject itself does not know what it really desires…'

A text pinged on her phone. She picked it up and looked at it. She groaned loudly, closed the magazine and turned over on the bed. He closed the book and lay down – face to face with her. He felt her warm breath on his face as he locked into the shimmering darkness of her green eyes and the oscillating rhythm of her pupils. He dared not look away, as if doing so would break the spell of that morning…but after a while it became apparent that her gaze went directly through him. She smiled and closed her eyes. The scene melted to darkness and re-emerged as brilliant white and beige, a pale blue wall, and down towards the bed a figure sat on a chair, dishevelled and with days of dark stubble.

His eyes crusted open. A voice spoke.

'Hud on a minute…there he is…Bobby Sands.'
'Awrite.' He replied weakly.
'Fuck sake man…canny leave you alone for a second.'

…

The bar in the project space, that night holding an exhibition, was busier than usual – the curator had brought along a crew of young organisers (aspiring duct-tapers, ushers and shushers) to busy themselves with various tasks; some stood handing out flyers and others walked around with catalogues, or asked the gathered attendees whether they required information. They performed their tasks with appropriate zeal, they eyed their colleagues suspiciously in-between bogus smiles exchanged as they passed each other, and through phonier requests which belied their intent as commands

– a rudimentary hierarchy jostled to establish itself, constantly collapsing then re-establishing; an atmosphere of vaunted ambition (in the service of paltry approbation) pervaded all of their actions. He observed this, and recorded it indifferently and only in passing – his main focus was now his own pain. In his still severely emaciated state, he could do nothing more than creak his wasted limbs, moving around the bar performing meagre actions slowly; ghostly pale – in clothes grown over-large and hung callously around an insufficient body – as if announcing in an indelicate scream the unnatural lack within. Everyone couldn't help but notice him, or to look at him pityingly, judgmentally and gratefully – filling in the details of the phantom terminal illness of their choosing, and thankful that they should be spared the experience of its wasting effects. His face was excuciantgly gaunt, the cheekbones jutted out; the skin sucked onto the contours of his jawbone – at one with images seen in only black and white in those remote exhibitions of atrocity. Although he had tried in the past few weeks to up his intake – and could feel his strength returning – the process was gradual and wearisome. After his discharge, he could do nothing more than sit in his room, leaving only to attend the mandated therapy sessions – which, he had found with some comfort, were just as unappealing as they had been in his earlier life. The pills were prescribed, and they accumulated – every week – in a pile of untouched boxes in a bag on his kitchen counter. And despite it all, the creaking limbs, the headaches; a weakness and corporeal vulnerability which he had before only felt in the abstract; the uneasiness with the process of digestion, and the clicking friction of his weary joints – he felt lucid. There was now an irrepressible and virile urge to grow, to bulk up – to become substantial, again. In the time he had spent under, he had reached and passed 30 years with the indifference and lack of ceremony that only the comatose are capable. It was an exhibition of large abstract paintings by a group of local artists. They were, by and large, derivative and with little merit – in some the colours, on first inspection, gave the eye an impression of unity…but lingering longer than a moment was sufficient to dismantle the illusion, all that was left was the spectacle of size, outsize expediency and viable ambition. It was art, in a manner of speaking…the art of being ruled. The opening had begun in the early evening, and by 10 it had begun to wind down. He chatted to customers, or indulged mundane questions and their interest, no doubt sparked through sympathy. People who he knew would drift in and out of his peripheries – some would be drawn into his orbit, only to tiptoe around the issue; others were repulsed entirely, held their heads down and averted their eyes. The performance began at half past ten. The lights dimmed and smoke descended onto the stage. A figure, an overweight woman, walked onto the stage… dressed in white lace panties, topless, her head covered in a white animal mask, half serpent and half bird – a long black beak hooked down from the nose, and a red lizard's tongue drooped down from it unconvincingly. She moved onto the stage and placed a black remote control, with an exaggerated red button, onto the edge of the stage. She tied herself to a chair and spread her legs. Her large pale body was covered in small pieces of chewing gum – sculpted into shapes that could only be discerned close-up. She began to speak; her accented voice disguised and distorted by electronic manipulation – robotic and inhuman.

'I have inserted something into myself. Something into my pussy. This button will activate it. Could I request someone to come forward…to engage it. To engage my suffering.'

As soon as she had said this, two of the helpers rushed forward with a practised unhurried gait towards the button – meeting at the front of the stage. There was a smiling exchange, until one relented. The red button was pushed with relish. A low level electronic buzzing filled the space – the PA system crackled, and the sound was amplified. The woman onstage began to writhe, slowly at first – building up gradually, with increasing intensity, until her entire body was gripped in huge convulsions. He couldn't take his eyes from the stage, at first – but eventually grew bored and let his eyes wander around room, and at the audience fixated on the spectacle, seemingly waiting for the appropriate moment when they, too, could simply avert their eyes. His limbs began to ache from over-exertion. He decided to take his break, unpinned his apron and headed towards the door. He stepped outside, collapsed into one of chairs beside the tables which looked out onto the street and closed his eyes. He felt himself nodding off.

'Oh…it didn't look like you were enjoying the performance.' He heard her voice say. He opened his eyes and glanced up. Her hair was longer now, and dyed blonde – but the face and the eyes were without change. She was breathing audibly and rapidly, her hands shaking slightly. She took a step towards him and then stopped. She smiled. She leaned her elbow awkwardly against the window to the side of the bench

'I saw you inside…I was trying to get your attention. You didn't see me, I guess.'

'Yeah…sorry. You look different.' He replied.

'I did it yesterday.'

'It's cool.'

'Oh thank you.'

'What's the performance?'

'Dunno…some girl from South America.'

He could feel her attempts to connect her eyes to his own, but he stubbornly kept his gaze focused on the taxis moving up and down the street. His head started to throb.

'How are you feeling?'

'I'm ok.'

'You look better.'

'Thanks.'

All at once he felt the sensation of an impending something…it began to swell up…but passed just as soon as he stopped the thought in its tracks. She began to speak but her voice stuttered, spluttered and broke. She sniffed loudly. He couldn't take his eyes off the road.

'I tried to see you a few times…but they wouldn't let me because I wasn't allowed to be there. He wouldn't let me either. I wanted to be there so much…if you can believe me. It was so horrible…I turned up one night and they told me to go home…and I just rushed passed them and went to your room…and I saw you on the bed. Just for a second.'

'…'

'I never knew you were so…If I could have just spoken to you, but I couldn't…I couldn't even try…or think about trying. Oh, I don't know. I saw you in that bed and I just wanted to climb in there…you just looked so…wounded.'

Across the road, a taxi driver got out, opened the passenger door, and unloaded a ramp which crashed onto a pavement with a metallic clank. An old man, dressed in a beige blazer – a panama hat pulled down to obscure his face – rolled his wheelchair forward. The taxi driver moved behind him and pushed the wheelchair up the ramp – a black Labrador followed them inside. The driver closed the door, stepped onto the pavement and lit a cigarette.

'I can't speak…I know…I can't speak, I don't know what to say…I just don't know how to express it right now…I thought I would, but I can't. And I should have spoken before…but I couldn't then either. But I wrote you letters…two letters. I can't write either…I guess I'm useless. But, I wrote everything in them… everything that I could write. I was going to give it to you on your birthday…but then this happened…and then I couldn't…and I wrote it again. I wrote another one. I wrote them both, I re-wrote them both – hundreds of times. My bin's full of paper…but I just wanted to give them to you.'

He took his eyes from the road, and briefly caught a glimpse of an arm placing two blue envelopes onto the table in front of him. They were made of quality watermarked paper, thick and full to bursting. He felt her linger, and heard the moist sucking sound of tears being wiped from eyelids…he closed his eyes and held his breath, and the presence, little by little, began to lessen and lessen – until he could feel it leave entirely. When he opened his eyes and glanced to his side, she was already gone.

Across the road, the taxi pulled out from the curb, and as it did so almost crashed into an oncoming car – which in turn swerved violently to avoid a collision. The car clipped a man waiting to cross the road on his side as he just managed to jump out of its path, landing face down on the concrete. Both drivers exited their vehicles and immediately ran to each other – a storm of steely expletives and impending violence echoing through the air. He leapt to his feet and ran towards the stricken man, lying senseless and prostrate on the pavement.

About the Author

Udith Dematagoda is a Scottish writer, academic and musician. Born in Sri Lanka in 1985, his family moved to Scotland and he grew up outside Edinburgh. Moving to Glasgow in 2004, he played guitar and sang in the post-punk band Un Cadavre, and finished a PhD in 2015. He is author of the monograph *Vladimir Nabokov and the Ideological Aesthetic*, and now lives and works in Tokyo. This is his first novel.